Lunch Ladies

Ruth O'Neil

Scripture quotations were taken from the Holy Bible, New International Version ®. Copyright 1973, 1978, 1984 International Bible Society. Used by permission of Zondervan.

Published by:
Books for Future Generations

Cover design by Ruth O'Neil
Cover photo by Bethany Tripp of Sunlit Portraits

ISBN: 978-1-7337307-6-1

Printed in the USA

Dedication

I have been so blessed over the years to have groups of women as close friends. When we do get together, it is often over food. Food is a great uniter of people, so it seemed natural to me to write about the Lunch Ladies as they gathered to share a meal. Some of those friends have been in my life for only a short time; others have been making the long haul beside me. I am grateful for all of them.

See the hands on that cover? Those hands are precious to me. This is not a stock photo. These are hands that have lifted me up in prayer during some of my most desperate times. When I asked one particular group of friends to share their hands with me for the photo, several commented that their hands looked old, were worn, had dry skin, had cuts and bruises. They didn't understand that their imperfect hands were perfect. These hands show that life is not always easy, but they show that together we can get through anything that comes our way as long as we have friends who will pray for us.

Prologue

$\mathcal{I}$ f these walls could talk, they would tell you sad stories, happy stories, silly stories, stories some people wish were not repeated...ever. They would tell you of grand plans never fulfilled. These stories would give you a picture of what true friendship is, even in all its imperfectness. These walls have seen tears, heard laughter, and kept secrets. Within these walls, some dreams came true, and some dreams were dashed to pieces.

Most of the walls were brick, the ones that weren't featured murals of local hotspots and people enjoying them. The artist did an exceptional job of creating people who seemed real. If one looked from just the right angle, the painted person popped right off the wall and seemed to sit at a table like any normal restaurant patron. If one was overly suspicious, these persons could be believed to be listening to every conversation whether private or not. Some of these painted onlookers could be perceived taking on an appropriate expression for the chatter taking place. They could appear to be happy, sad, or even surprised, but never uninterested.

It is in the shadows of these murals a group of friends meet. These are the walls of the 316 Bistro. The first Monday of every month is important for seven friends. That's lunch day. Nothing interrupts lunch day.

Chapter 1

Be devoted to one another in love. Honor one another above yourselves. Never be lacking in zeal, but keep your spiritual fervor, serving the Lord. - Romans 12:10-11

September

Ryann (Little Leader)

"Where's Paige?" Ryann was ready to pray for their lunch, but Paige had come up missing. Even though Paige had a tendency to run late, she had arrived on time today.

"I'm sorry," Paige came rushing up to the table and sat in her seat. "I was in the bathroom talking to myself. I thought I was alone, but I wasn't. I made a new friend though."

Ryann just shook her head and smiled. Paige was a friendly sort. She could make friends anywhere, anytime, sometimes in the strangest of places. Obviously.

A little bit later, once everyone had received their food and were intent on eating, Ryann looked down at the food on her plate. *I should have ordered a salad*, she thought to herself. The greasy burger and fries weren't doing much for her already upset stomach. This had been a common problem lately, and she had no idea why. The last time she had an upset stomach for more than one day in a row was when she was pregnant. However, she knew that wasn't the case. The youngest of her four daughters was twelve and the oldest was in her second year of college. Being pregnant would be a cruel joke at this point in her life.

Then there was the fact that her husband had been killed in a car accident more than five years ago. She hadn't so much as looked at a man since. She knew she would never remarry feeling it would ruin what she and her husband had had for so many years. She was fine being on her own. Yes, it had been hard, especially at first, but her girls were the greatest daughters ever. Even while they were grieving about their father's sudden passing, they stepped up to the plate and were helpful in more ways than she could count. She couldn't help but smile whenever she thought of them. Ryann recalled the many times people asked if she was babysitting her little sisters. She had always been petite and younger looking than her true age. Her long brown hair helped with that. She often wore it in a simple braid down her back and out of her face, as she liked to say. As of yet, not one gray hair had shown itself, but when it did, Ryann vowed to give it a good yank and promptly flush it down the toilet. Looking at herself in the mirror, Ryann had only ever seen a nondescript female. For the most part, she was able to blend in and be invisible, but then there were her eyes.

Although she tried to hide her feelings, she knew her eyes always gave her away. Her green eyes were her best feature, at least most days. Then there were the days those eyes betrayed her. Normally her eyes were brilliant, emerald green, the problem was, like many people with green eyes, her eyes had a tendency to change color. Sometimes the color appeared to change because of the clothes she was wearing, but other times her eyes changed color because of her mood or her health. When her eyes looked more blue or gray, there was no hiding from her family or close friends that she was either angry or not feeling well.

This morning when she had gotten dressed, she noticed her eyes had that blue-gray tint. Because she didn't want any of her friends asking questions, she tried on several shirts to force her eyes back to green, but nothing had worked.

Mercedes, one of her lunch lady friends who was sitting next to her, leaned over and discreetly whispered, "Are you not feeling well again?"

She should have known there would be no fooling or hiding anything from Mercedes. Mercedes and Ryann had been best friends since first grade. Ryann had been the new girl at school, and her mother had not known to pack an extra snack. When snack time came around, Mercedes had noticed and scooched her chair right next to Ryann so they could share her snack. They had been inseparable ever since, except for the few teenage years when Mercedes was busy doing her own thing. Mercedes knew Ryann better than anyone else. No, there were no secrets kept from Mercedes.

Ryann sort of smiled and nodded.

"Are you ever going to the doctor's?"

Ryann tried to laugh and brush it off a little bit. "I'm just not as young as I used to be. Greasy foods bother me now which only emphasizes the fact that I should have ordered a salad."

"You should have gone to the doctor a while ago," Mercedes whispered so no one else could hear their conversation.

"I have gone to the doctor." Ryann knew her mimicking voice was rude, but she was not in the mood for Mercy to be her usual motherly self.

Mercedes sighed. "Let me rephrase my question. Did you go to another doctor to get a second opinion, or did you just take the word of the first doctor because he told you what you wanted to hear?"

Ryann glared at Mercedes. Why wouldn't she just leave her alone?

Mercedes must have been able to sense Ryann's disappointment/anger/something, because she just laid a hand on Ryann's leg under the table, out of sight of everyone else, and gave it a squeeze as if to apologize.

Ryann tried to force a smile in Mercy's direction. She took a deep breath and grabbed Mercy's hand and squeezed back to let her know that all was forgiven. Ryann knew her friend meant well. There was none so loyal as Mercedes.

Mercedes (Merciful)

Mercedes kept an eye on Ryann throughout their lunch while still conversing with the rest of the group. With all of her concern over Ryann, she was able to take her mind off her own issues, even if just for a short time. She would much rather spend her time worrying over the situation Ryann was in that she couldn't help, over the situation her daughter Annie got herself in on purpose. Not to mention the strained relationship between mother and daughter that was growing worse each day. But Mercedes was truly worried about Ryann, and Ryann didn't seem to be taking things seriously. The issues had been going on for quite some time now, and it looked like Ryann's face was getting a little thinner. Ryann had no weight to lose. She was all of "four-foot-nine and a half" she liked to say. She maybe weighed a hundred pounds soaking wet before, when she liked to eat. Mercedes had had her own share of health issues in the past, and she felt there was something more wrong with Ryann than a simple upset stomach as she said.

Tinkling on glass pulled Mercedes from her troubling thoughts. She looked up to see Mackenzie standing at the head of the table with a glass and a fork in her hand. Since Mackenzie was so soft-spoken, making noise that was louder than her voice was the only way she could get everyone's attention.

Of course, to strangers, Mackenzie easily stood out of the crowd. She was six-foot-two and in her own words was "built like a linebacker." People often took a second look when they spied her. However, it was often a second and possibly a third time that people had to ask her to repeat herself when she spoke because she was so quiet. Mack's voice didn't quite match up with her appearance. With this group of ladies all cackling like hens at the same time, there was no other way for her to get everyone's attention than to tap her glass.

Mercedes inwardly groaned. She knew exactly what was about to happen. It happened every year at this same time ever since they had started their lunch ladies group.

It was her birthday, and Mackenzie was going to make a big deal of it. Mercedes didn't know why she felt singled out; Mackenzie did the same theatrical presentation for each birthday in the group. Everyone knew to automatically start singing "Happy Birthday," another thing Mercedes didn't care for. For some reason, it always made her feel like crawling under a rock and hiding out of sight. But, there were no rocks large enough or handy enough to conceal her, so she just had to grin and bear it graciously.

Mackenzie (Teacher)

After the singing had died down, Mackenzie handed Mercedes a rather large wrapped package.

"Happy birthday, Mercy," Mackenzie said, giving her friend as big a hug as she could around the package.

"Thanks, Mack."

Mackenzie waited in anxious anticipation as Mercedes opened the gift ever so slowly. Mackenzie put a lot of thought, time, and effort into the gifts she gave her friends. It took even greater effort for her to wait to give her gifts at the appropriate time. She was almost giddy. She twisted her dirty blonde hair with her left hand while she chomped on the nails of her right hand as she stood there, watching and waiting.

Oh, Mack! It's absolutely perfect!"

Mackenzie looked over Mercedes' shoulder as she took in her work again. She had taken pictures and made a scrapbook type framed collage. It had taken a while, but she had managed to put hers and Mercedes' relationship all within the confines of a frame.

"Thanks, Mack." Mercedes put down the frame and gave Mackenzie a proper hug. "I don't know how you find the time to do all you do."

While Mackenzie still had a smile pasted on her face, her inner demeanor lost its smile. Mercedes truly didn't mean anything by her comment, but it was a reminder of Mackenzie's life. Her life was less than perfect.

She had married "that man", her present name for her ex-husband, who she thought was the love of her life, right out of high school. Not long after she found herself pregnant. Shortly after she gave birth to Jordan, she realized "that man" wasn't the prince she thought he was. He was lazy, couldn't hold down a job, and couldn't care less about her or Jordan.

No matter how hard she tried, she couldn't make "that man" love her. She knew she had gained a little weight after they had gotten married, which she blamed on having a baby, dealing with a lot of stress in her life, and simply the fact she wasn't a teenager anymore. Eventually, she quit trying as none of her efforts at anything made a difference. She vowed to never have another baby who would grow up in that environment. But then, ten years into the marriage, she found herself pregnant again. When she told "that man", he up and left saying there was no way the baby was his. Mackenzie never saw him again, except in divorce court. That was finalized two years ago. Now she did everything on her own. Child support was non-existent. She could have used the courts to chase the louse down for money, but then he might fight for visitation or even custody. She figured her boys were better off without him. She certainly was. It wasn't that he cared enough about the boys to fight for custody; it was his hatred for her and knowing how much pain it would inflict that would be his reasoning for the battle.

Cameron had never known his father who hadn't even bothered to show up when Cameron was born.

Thinking of Cameron reminded Mackenzie of the trouble he had coming. No one really knew what was wrong with him. She even had one doctor tell her that Cameron was going to die before he was ten years old, and there was nothing she could do about it. She didn't go back to that doctor. She could only sit back and watch Cameron suffer. She must have done something at some point in her life to make God so angry with her that He would threaten to take her son away. But Cameron's smile was something she looked forward to every day. He was such a happy little boy, and it broke her heart to pieces to wonder if she really had such a short time to be his mom.

These once a month lunches with the ladies from church were an escape. An older lady from church, who happened to live next door, stayed with Cam for free telling Mackenzie she needed to get away once in a while. Lunch allowed her to temporarily forget all of her troubles. Each one of the ladies around this table was so precious to her. She also knew each one had her own battles she was fighting.

She looked up and her eyes connected with Angela.

Angela (Giver)

"That's absolutely gorgeous, Mack!" Angela said after she had passed Mercedes' gift along the table. "I look at mine every day. I think I see something new every time I look at it."

Angela was a feisty redhead. She had the most confidence of all the women in the group and carried herself as such, although she knew it was all a farce. She really had no confidence. While almost everyone around her was long ago married, not Angela. She had been searching for the love of her life for all of her life, at least that's the way it seemed.

She couldn't help but tear up a little when she saw pictures of the other ladies with their children. She was not exactly jealous of these women and their families; she wasn't sure what she would call it either. She was confident God had a plan for her; she just wished He'd hurry up and let her in on it.

Angela knew she could never have children, and that was actually okay with her. Being almost forty years old she had come to terms with that. That fact actually helped her when it came to her non-pending marriage. There was no biological clock ticking for her.

When she was a young girl, she had great plans to go to the mission field. Her parents had missionaries coming and going from their home all the time when Angela was growing up. Her father had built a little cabin in the woods behind their house so missionaries their church supported would have a free and quiet place to stay while on furlough, a little retreat from the busyness and stress that came with full-time ministry.

These families would often eat dinner with Angela and her family. Around the dinner table was where she heard exciting story after story about God at work. Angela wanted to be part of that. Her plan had always been to go to the mission field with a partner, a husband, who could share the work with her, and they could be supportive of each other. When a husband never came into her life, going to the mission field became less of a priority for her. Now, instead of going to the mission field herself, she sent her money there. She also sat on a mission's board and helped those who were on the field any way she could.

For many years her life's prayer was one for discernment. She always wanted to know where there was a true need she could do something about. God often opened her eyes and showed her things she couldn't possibly know otherwise. Sometimes someone would say they had a need, but then God would show Angela how that person was either not helping himself or that the request was not truly a need. Angela had learned to listen to the voice of God over the years. When she felt the now familiar tug on her heartstrings, she knew God was sending her a message. Other times she had a different feeling, and that one meant to steer clear

"By the way, Aunt Angela."

Angela lifted her head to look at Zena sitting across the table from her.

Zena (Hospitality)

"My kids love that cookbook you bought them. They have been fighting over it so much, I've had to come up with a kitchen rotation!" Zena said in her accented voice.

"I'm glad they've enjoyed it. I figured you would fit it into your homeschooling schedule somehow," Angela answered.

"I appreciate it too. The forced schedule gives me one-on-one time with each of them. It's a precious time to me."

Zena truly appreciated Angela and her friendship. Although Angela had no children of her own, she had adopted all six of Zena's as her nieces and nephews, often bringing them little gifts such as the cookbook and spending time with them whenever she could. At Zena's happy thoughts about Angela, baby number seven jumped around inside her belly.

She put her hand on her belly and smiled at the life growing within. Fifteen years ago she never would have thought she would be here now. Born and raised in Greece, her life had been what some would have called enchanting simply because of location, but it was far from perfect. There were things about her life that even these ladies, her closest friends, didn't know. Absentmindedly, she put her hands on her arms to make sure her ever-present long sleeves were in place.

But now, Zena had melded into life in America. Somehow she had become the quintessential homeschooling mom, right down to the denim skirts and canvas sneakers. While others might tease about them, she just found them practical and comfortable. She could go from feeding the chickens, to teaching, to cooking and preserving food, to working in the garden all without having to change her clothes or worry if she was going to ruin something. Except for her Greek accent, she knew she was a little stereotypical, but she didn't care. She had found a wonderful and supporting husband in Cooper. He made her feel beautiful every day of her life, and she would never take him for granted.

"You guys want to hear something funny?"

Zena heard Paige groan, but Zena didn't care. She had no shortage of funny kid stories, and she liked to share them since they made people laugh. Someday when Paige had children of her own with silly stories to tell, then she would understand, and Zena would be there to listen to Paige tell every single one of them. At least the rest of the lunch ladies enjoyed her story of the month, as they had come to call it.

"We started school a couple of weeks ago, and I was excited to get little Sadie all started on her first day of kindergarten. She brought me a book and asked if we could read it before we began. Of course I always want to encourage my kids to read, so I said we could. She plopped herself down at her new desk, opened the book up, and began reading like she had already been reading for years!"

"How did she manage that?" Ryann wondered.

"About the time I figured something was up, I heard snickering behind me. I turned around and caught Sarah and Sophie trying not to laugh. Apparently, they wanted to surprise me, and they had been teaching Sadie all summer long."

"That's so sweet!" Mercedes said.

"Sounds like you have some budding teachers on your hands!" Mackenzie smiled.

Paige (Servant)

Paige rolled her eyes. It seemed that every single month Zena had some new sweet, cute, or funny story to tell about her kids. Paige didn't find most of them amusing.

Changing the subject she asked, "So, Zena, when are you going to pop out this next Pez?" This was not something

Paige would say to anyone else. She was teasing, and she knew Zena knew that.

Zena proved it by smiling and looking lovingly at her protruding belly. "Not long now. Maybe another month or so."

Paige loved Zena's accent. When she was a child she would practice voices in different accents. She always thought she should have gotten a job in voice-over work, but it never happened. Instead, she found herself in the completely unglamorous job of stuffing envelopes. Not that she was ungrateful for the job though. It allowed her to work at home where she was her grandmother's caregiver. That saved her grandmother a ton of money on in-home nurses or worse yet, a retirement home. Not having a job outside of the house saved money on clothes and makeup as well. Paige never really cared about that stuff anyway. She rather liked the frumpy look. Between Paige's income and her grandmother's pension, they were doing just fine financially. They were not rich by any means, but the bills were paid, and there was food on the table. Paige's second choice of career would definitely have been matchmaker. She just had not thought of how she could make it work. Thoughts of matchmaking reminded her of something

Turning her attention to Angela, she said. "Oh, Ang, I forgot to tell you, I met this really nice guy last week—"

"No," Angela held up her hand before Paige could continue.

Paige and Angela had been friends for quite a while, despite the difference in their ages. Paige felt she knew Angela better than anyone else and was constantly using that information to try and set her up on blind dates, which had been one failure after another.

"They say that couples who go on blind dates are more likely to have a happy, healthy marriage." Paige opened her eyes wide in her seriousness.

Angela stared at her for a moment. "Who's 'they'?"

"A couple of relationship experts I've been following on social media. I'm sure they did their research and know it's true."

"I'm sure you have more to worry about with your grandma than setting me up with pitiful dates," Angela said.

Paige did have plenty to do. Her grandmother, the woman who raised her, was frail and needed almost constant care. When Paige had originally heard of her grandmother's need, she was more than willing to move into Grammy's home and return the favor.

She ignored Angela's implication and added, "You're supposed to meet him Friday night at seven. Same place as usual."

"Maybe if you changed the location of these fiascoes, it might be helpful. I'm beginning to think that restaurant has a bad aura about it."

Paige chose to ignore Angela and once again, her ADD attention scooted from one person to another. "Oh, Kayleigh, there was something I wanted to ask you to pray about?"

Kayleigh (Warrior)

"What's that?"

Kayleigh was the newest member of the lunch ladies group. She had attended the church for less than six months, but she had already proven herself as a prayer warrior. Kayleigh appeared to be an average 32-year-old blond woman. Her mild-mannered ways fit exactly with her perfect appearance. She worked at what the rest of the ladies called "a fancy woman's dress shop." She did always have to dress the part. It gave her the look of having been raised in a proper home, been taught impeccable etiquette, her hair always flawlessly in place, but it was all a lie. Her life was a mess, and she had shared very little of it with these women with whom she was now sharing a meal. They knew she was a prayer warrior, but they didn't fully understand the extent of the circumstances that caused her to be.

"All right, Paige, what's your request?"

"Angela here needs a man." Paige looked sideways at Angela and winked. "Could you pray that God will bring her the perfect one?"

Although Kayleigh knew Paige was teasing…somewhat, she also knew there was a sincerity to the request.

"Oh, I'd be glad to add her to my list." Kayleigh pulled out the little black book she carried around with her for the sole purpose of writing down prayer requests. She never wanted to forget what people asked her to pray for. "Angela is on my list," she said putting the top back on her pen.

"Great!" Angela threw her hands up in the air. "Now I'll be married within a year."

Everyone at the table laughed. They all knew God took Kayleigh's prayers seriously.

"All right, everyone."

Kayleigh turned as Ryann hollered to get everyone's attention before they parted ways. "Same time, same place next month." Ryann glanced down at her watch and added, "I have to get back to the bank. Last month I was a little late returning, and my boss wasn't too happy about it."

Lunch time was over for another month. It didn't look like Kayleigh would be telling them any of her secrets today, in spite of the fact that she felt a desperate need to share her burden with someone…anyone.

Chapter 2

And let us consider how we may spur one another on toward love and good deeds, not giving up meeting together, as some are in the habit of doing, but encouraging one another – and all the more as you see the day approaching.– Hebrews 10:24-25

October

Mercedes

"Now I can eat whatever I want for lunch, can't I?" Mackenzie asked Mercedes only half joking.

"Not exactly," Mercedes answered back.

"Come on, Mercedes…"

"You know I hate being called that."

"Yes, I know, but it sounds so sophisticated."

"Then why do you continue to do it if you know I hate it?"

"Because I want to eat whatever I want for lunch, *Mercy*." Mackenzie put emphasis on her friend's preferred nickname.

"Fine. You can eat whatever you want. Just don't come crying to me when you don't lose the few pounds you're trying to."

"You are named wrong. You don't have any mercy."

Mercedes smirked. "I do when it's warranted. You can't walk a mile and then eat cheesecake while drinking a soda and hope your little walk helped."

Mercedes and Mackenzie had been walking a couple of days a week all summer long. With summer gone and fall coming to a close soon, not to mention the rainy weather plaguing the area lately, they had not had a whole lot of time to walk, hence their reason for walking to lunch.

This was a time Mercedes had come to enjoy. It gave her an opportunity to get to know the shy Mackenzie. In a group, Mackenzie didn't talk much, but one-on-one she had been much more eager to share some of the things that were going on in her life.

Mercedes wished she could share some of it with the rest of the group, but she had a feeling that if she ever betrayed Mack's confidence it would be the end of their friendship. That was a chance Mercedes was not willing to take.

Mercedes smiled as Mackenzie loudly blew air out of her mouth. She patted her friend on the back. "Let's just enjoy this beautiful weather. This is probably one of the last nice days we will have before the weather turns cold."

They silently finished the remainder of the walk to the restaurant. Mercedes figured silence was best. Mackenzie was doing some heavy breathing and was finding it difficult to speak. Besides, Mercedes had plenty to think about in the quiet.

Mercedes was one of the oldest ladies in the group, tied only with Ryann. But for some reason, the rest of them looked up to her as a mother figure. Perhaps it was because of the rough life she had lived for a time. She had certainly gained some wisdom from that time period in her life. The motherly impression could have also come from the fact that she was a grandmother – three times over. A grandma gave the impression of age, but that wasn't necessarily true in her case. Whatever the reasoning for her position in the group, Mercedes was okay with it. She would gladly pass on the wisdom she had gained to try and keep others from making the same mistakes she had.

If only her daughter, Annie, would be so wise.

At least with these women, her advice was usually taken, if not seriously considered. It made her feel like less of a failure with the choices her own daughter was making, in spite of Mercedes' past experiences and advice.

Mercedes looked forward to the chatter of her dear friends. This one day a month allowed her to put her own personal problems on the back burner. Several others in the group had much worse issues than an unruly daughter who insisted on making bad choices.

Now that she had officially retired by the age of forty-five, she found she had a lot of time to think, maybe too much time. Maybe a super early retirement wasn't such a good thing. She felt she was on the borderline of overanalyzing everything in her life. Ah! Who was she kidding? Mercedes knew she had stepped over that boundary long ago. Her life had never been perfect, she knew that. She had no problem admitting the mistakes she had made. But beyond that were nagging feelings that her mistakes caused all the problems she was having with Annie. Mercedes felt everything was her fault. Annie was the way she was because Mercedes was her mother.

Although she wasn't sure exactly where it was in the Bible, she knew there was a verse that said something about the sins of the father being passed on to the children. Yep. She was fairly certain her sins had messed up Annie's life.

Mercedes had worked hard all her life. Even after so many of her mistakes, she had found a good job as a delivery truck driver. She enjoyed the work and being on the road. The pay was really good, and she was home each night, albeit late at night. At the time she thought she was doing what was best for her and Annie. Later she realized that being home with Annie more would have been beneficial to say the least. Because Mercedes wasn't home much, Annie had to find ways to entertain herself. That entertainment usually came in the form of boys. By age fifteen Annie was expecting her first baby. Mercedes had thought taking care of the baby might help keep Annie from getting into more trouble. Mercedes did what she could to help, but she allowed most of the responsibility to fall to Annie. With the baby and school, Mercedes thought Annie would be too tired for "extracurricular activities." She was wrong once again. Two more babies followed in quick succession. Eventually, Annie and the kids moved out of the house to live with the current boyfriend.

Mercedes hated for her grandchildren to live that kind of a life, but there really wasn't much she could do. Annie hardly ever spoke to her anymore. Mercedes only rarely saw the grandkids. She despised the thought that the oldest seemed to be following in her mother's and her grandmother's footsteps.

If Mercedes had made better choices, maybe Annie would have too.

Mackenzie

Mackenzie was never so glad to see the restaurant finally come into view. It only took two minutes to drive there, but when she was walking it felt so very, very, very far away.

As soon as she and Mercedes entered, she found their table and plopped down in a chair. She didn't think she would ever catch her breath. She hadn't known she could sweat so much. And what was the smell? Oh, wait. It was her. Maybe walking to lunch wasn't such a good idea anymore. She certainly didn't want to offend those who sat around the table with her. She knew she hated it when she had to wait on someone at her own waitressing job who smelled less than pleasant.

Mackenzie sighed with pleasure when the waitress put a cold glass of water in front of her. How good it felt to be waited on. Once a month she was the one who got to sit and relax. Waiting tables wasn't her idea of a great job, but the tips could be good and that helped ease her financial burden, at least a little bit.

Between raising two boys by herself and the numerous trips to the doctor's office with Cameron, money was extremely tight. Then there were the groceries. Jordan had hit twelve years old and was constantly eating. She didn't know where he put it all. She started grocery shopping while he was at school so she could hide some of them to ration them out. She knew she was tall and "that man" was tall. It was more than likely that Jordan would be tall as well. The problem was that she wasn't sure she could afford to keep feeding him until he was eighteen. Maybe she would have to see about getting him a job at the restaurant soon. Working there one shift would feed him one meal. That would help some. Except for the fact that he was only twelve and couldn't legally work for several years yet.

"Did you know that having good friends and getting together with them on a regular basis prolongs your life more than exercise will?" Paige's voice harshly interrupted Mackenzie's thoughts.

Mackenzie turned and looked at Paige with questions in her eyes. "What?"

"It's true. I read that online somewhere."

Mackenzie turned her head back to face forward. She would've given it a shake out of frustration, but she wasn't sure she had that much energy left after the walk. Then she made a face to herself while she was deep in thought. Maybe Paige was onto something. Good friends did raise one's spirits.

Then again, friends might help one's emotional state, but getting together once a month at a restaurant where Mackenzie was in love with the rolls, might be a part of her weight issues.

Mackenzie took a deep breath. She always looked forward to this time. She needed to be with friends who lifted her up.

But first, she needed to use the ladies' room. If she could smell herself, she figured those around her could too.

"I'll be right back."

Fortunately, no one was in the bathroom. She pumped the bar on the paper towel holder several times to get a decent amount of paper. After wetting the paper towels and putting some soap on them, she snuck into one of the stalls.

How embarrassing would it be if someone walked in here while I was washing my armpits?

Looking down she thought it might be a good idea to take a swipe at her cleavage too. It looked pretty sweaty. As she was disposing of her paper towels outside the stall, her eyes landed on a wall-mounted hand sanitizer. It only took her a moment to determine alcohol may not be deodorant, but it was the next best thing she had at the moment. One pump into her hand quickly went under one arm and then a second pump into her other hand went under the other arm. After a quick wash of her hands, she was more or less presentable enough to be in the company of others.

Mackenzie made it back to the table just in time for the waitress to take her order.

"Shall we begin?" Ryann asked as soon as the waitress walked away. Without a word from the others, they all took hold of the hand of the lady beside her, forming an unbroken circle around the table.

"Dear heavenly Father, once again we come before You to ask You to bless our friendship and bless the food we are about to eat. I thank You that we have been able to gather together. Amen."

Each voice around the table chorused Ryann's amen.

"How's your son doing, Mack?" Kayleigh asked as she put a bite of food in her mouth.

"Keep praying for him. He has another cold. We are barely even into cold and flu season. I don't know where he keeps picking things up. It's not like I have him in daycare or anything."

"Jordan could be bringing germs home from school," Zena suggested.

"But Jordan hasn't been sick."

Kayleigh shrugged her shoulders. "That doesn't mean he isn't bringing home germs. You could try making Jordan shower and change his clothes as soon as he gets home before he gets anywhere near Cameron."

Mackenzie bobbed her head back and forth. "I hadn't thought of that. It might be worth a try."

"If that doesn't work, let me know," Zena piped in. "I can mix up some of my herbs and oils. I make my kids take them all the time and we hardly ever get sick in our house."

"Is there anything that can help boost his immune system?" Mackenzie wondered. "He's been sick so much that I imagine his immune system is weakened and hasn't had a chance to catch up."

"Oh, sure. I'll bring some to church on Sunday. Or do you want them sooner?"

Mackenzie nodded her head toward Zena's belly. "I don't think you need to do any extra driving around right now. I can grab them Sunday."

Mackenzie silently prayed for her little boy, as she often did when he came to her mind. He was so tiny, and his sweet little face made her smile. She just wanted him to be healthy like his big brother. If she was completely open and honest with herself, she wished for his good health to help alleviate the medical bills. It seemed she had him at the doctor every other week lately. Her insurance co-pay was only twenty dollars each time, but then there were the prescriptions on top of that. A few times she had been able to get a free sample, either from the doctor or from the pharmaceutical company, but finances were still strained. She would do anything to help her son; however, her financial affairs were becoming desperate. If it weren't for the cash she received in the mail every once in a while, she didn't know what she would do.

For months she had tried to put a name to the anonymous benefactor. She really didn't think it was the boys' dad. "That man" would have to put someone else's needs before his own. If he was sending money, he would be loudly proclaiming it. She considered it could be her own parents, but then she ruled them out as well. Mackenzie knew exactly what their stance had been on her marriage and leaving home.

Then there were "that man's" parents. However, they had never really been a huge fan of Mackenzie. The only reason Mackenzie thought about them was because they did have the money and maybe they felt a little bit sorry for her for the way their son had treated her and abandoned his children. Then again, if they had been that concerned they might have come around to see the boys once in a while themselves. Mackenzie would never have denied them access to their grandsons.

Paige

"Hey, everyone, I forgot. I have the greatest news to share with you because sharing good news with friends is the best. I learned that this morning from one of the blogs I follow."

"What is it?" Ryann asked, ignoring the blog comment.

Paige could hardly contain herself. "Guess who I got an email from?"

"Who?" Everyone asked at the same time.

Paige paused long enough to make sure she had everyone's attention. When all eyes were on her she answered. "My brother."

Silence filled the room.

"Brother?" Mercedes questioned. "Since when do you have a brother?"

"Ever since I was born. He's several years older than me."

"What did he want?" Angela's face showed concern.

"How did he find you?" Zena and Angela asked the question at the same time.

Paige held up her hands to signify she would explain everything. "I always knew I had a brother because Grammy would tell me stories about him. She gave me a picture of him once, and I've kept it ever since dreaming of meeting him one day. You see, my parents divorced when I was only a year old. My mom ran off with me, and I haven't seen my dad or my brother since. Then when I was two, my mom died, leaving Grammy to raise me. She never knew where my father and brother went.

"Anyway, my brother has supposedly been looking for me for years. He said it was a fluke he found me at all. Apparently, my mom changed our names when she ran away because she no longer wanted anything to do with my dad."

"So, what's he like?"

"Have you met him?"

"When do we get to meet him?"

Paige knew she wasn't answering the ladies' questions fast enough.

"I'm getting there; there's a lot to tell." She took a deep breath and continued. "He's been living somewhere in Africa, I forget exactly where he said, as a missionary."

"How wonderful!" Kayleigh exclaimed. "He must know the Lord as well."

Paige's smile was huge. "He does. He's here in the US, and we are meeting sometime next week."

Kayleigh put her hand on top of Paige's. "I'll be praying for you. I'll pray that your reunion is wonderful. Everything you ever dreamed it would be."

Paige smiled at the godly woman sitting next to her and clasped her hand. She was so thankful for such friends, even though there were times she felt like the annoying little sister.

Angela

"I wanted to be a missionary when I was a child," Angela told the group, her heart once again hurting because her plans to be a missionary had not worked out.

"Really?" Mackenzie asked.

"Yes. A missionary nurse to be exact. My mother even sewed me a nurse costume when I was a little girl."

"Your mom knew how to sew?" Kayleigh questioned.

"She was a wonderful seamstress," Angela smiled at the memories of all the beautiful dresses her mother had made her.

"And she didn't pass any of that along to you?" Paige teased.

Angela took the rib good-naturedly. "Believe me, it's not because she didn't try. My poor mother. Eventually, she just gave up on me."

"You would have to give up all the nice things you have if you were a missionary," Paige commented.

Angela shrugged her shoulders. "It's just stuff. None of it means anything. God gave it to me, and God could take it away at any moment. Possessions never really meant much to me. I'd give it all up if it meant I could have a family of my own or give purpose to my life. If God asked me to give up all my material possessions I owned so I could serve Him better, I would do it in a heartbeat."

The ladies were silent for a moment as if digesting what Angela said. Silence was a rarity for them and here it happened twice in one meal.

Then Mercedes broke that silence. "How come you never went to the mission field?"

Angela shrugged again. "I felt it was more something I wanted. I never felt God calling me to it. Some things needed to fall into place first, and they just never did."

"At least not yet," added Kayleigh, ever the encourager.

Angela smiled. "Right. At least not yet. I guess that's why I've enjoyed being on the mission board. It uses my time for a good cause. I can help support missionaries who need an extra financial boost, and I can still be involved in missions. I truly believe God has kept me where I am so I can offer both prayer and financial support for missionary friends."

"And you think your life has no purpose." Mackenzie quietly made a statement rather than asking a question.

Angela understood. She sent a private smile of understanding to her friend. Then Angela bowed her head and smiled to herself. Maybe her life had been purposeful all along, and she had just never realized it.

Zena

"Oh, boy! I don't mean to interrupt your sweet story, Angela, or break up this party, but I think I may need to get myself to the hospital!" Zena was holding her belly with both hands.

"Are you having contractions?" Angela was immediately by Zena's side.

"Better than that," Zena answered. "My water just broke."

Suddenly, all of the ladies pushed their chairs back and stood up, some knocking their chairs over. They all started talking at once.

The waitress came over after hearing all the commotion. "Is everything okay?" she asked

"Could we get checks quickly, please? Zena's water broke."

The manager had been in another part of the dining room and must have overheard what happened because he came over all excited. "Go! Go! Lunch is on us today."

Angela was helping Zena get up. As they walked by the manager, Angela said, "Thank you. We'll make it up to you."

"You're faithful regulars. There's nothing to make up. We're having a baby!" He seemed just as excited as everyone else.

"Are we all going to the hospital?" Mackenzie wondered.

"Of course we are," Ryann said a little louder than she meant to.

"We can all fit in my van," Zena said. Then she decided to add, "As long as someone else is willing to drive." Zena tossed her purse to Mackenzie. "The keys are in there."

Everyone piled into Zena's fifteen-passenger van while Angela helped Zena into the front seat and the rest of them piled in the back.

"How do you even sit here?" Mackenzie asked as she looked at the front seat and its closeness to the steering wheel.

Zena looked at her in exasperation. "I'm a whole lot shorter than you are. I need to be able to reach the pedals."

"But what about your big fat belly? How do you fit that in here?" Mackenzie was still standing outside of the van, gesturing to the minimal space between the seat and the steering wheel.

"Just get in the van and drive," Angela hollered from one of the middle seats after settling Zena and herself.

Zena watched as Mackenzie wrestled with the seat to try get it to go back far enough so she would be comfortable driving. After about three contractions she had had enough. "Mackenzie, just get in the van and drive now!"

"Okay, okay. Don't get your knickers in a knot." Mackenzie struggled to get into the van with her long legs and the seat still too far forward.

"Take a left out of the parking lot," Zena felt the need to give directions, but at the same time caught herself. "I'm sorry, Mackenzie. I'm so used to bossing kids around that I'm bossing you now."

"That's all right," Mackenzie responded. "I do know how to get to the hospital, but if it helps you to give me directions, you go right ahead."

Mack stepped on the gas pedal in the van lurched forward. Then she hit a speedbump and stomped on the brakes rather hard. The ladies in the back of the van all gasped and hung on for dear life.

"We're never going to get there!" Paige whined from the back.

"I don't really want to have this baby in the van," Zena's voice went up an octave from the beginning of her statement to the end.

"It sure is clean enough to," Mercedes spoke up from the rear of the van.

"Yes, don't you have like six kids? How come your van is so clean?" Paige added her two cents.

"Oooohhh!" Zena wailed in response. Then when the contraction subsided she said, "I'm OCD, and I passed that along to my kids. I worked hard to teach them that a mess isn't good."

She stopped abruptly as another contraction overtook her. She held her breath.

"These are pretty close together," Ryann stated.

Mackenzie stepped on the gas a little too hard again, giving those in the back only minor whiplash. There were more gasps from the back.

"Sorry! I'm sitting too close to the pedals," she apologized into the rearview mirror.

"Don't worry about me!" Zena held up her hand. "I'm fine." She was more than a little sarcastic.

"Yeah!" Paige shouted from the back of the van. "Don't worry about me either, even though I have a tendency to get motion sickness."

"Hold it in, Paige," Zena was able to holler back between contractions. "Do not throw up in my van!"

"I'll try not to." A moment later, "I need some air. How do you open the windows back here?"

"You don't." Zena was able to spit out those two words in the middle of a contraction.

"I'm going to be sick!"

"Shut up!" The passengers in the back shouted at Paige in unison.

Zena couldn't help but smile at the chorus of shouts. She was the one in labor, but apparently, Paige was getting on everyone else's nerves as well.

Just as another contraction was doing its work, Mackenzie rounded a corner and screeched into the hospital parking lot. Everyone reached for the nearest handhold as she stepped on the brake a little harder than necessary.

Zena felt the need to push, especially after Mackenzie's driving.

"I'll get you a wheelchair," Angela said as she gladly hopped out of the van first.

"I'll go and notify them you're here," Ryann jumped out of the van next.

"I'm going to try and get out of here," Mackenzie was struggling to get her tall frame out of the moved-up-way-too-far driver's seat.

Zena waited as patiently as she could while the other ladies piled out of the car.

"I lost my shoe," Paige shouted.

Mercedes found it and kicked it out of the van toward Paige, who was hopping on one foot. Zena watched Paige hop as the shoe went a little off course. It would have been almost comical if she wasn't trying desperately to hold the baby in. Laughter would not have been good at that moment. Then again, neither was even the thought of jumping up and down.

When Angela came back with a wheelchair she asked, "Can you step down okay?"

"I'm afraid to," Zena said.

"Is something wrong?" Angela wondered.

"I'm afraid if I move the baby is going to fall out."

"Maybe if you didn't have so many babies..." Paige began, but the immediate looks of the other ladies stopped her from finishing her sentence. That and Kayleigh's punch to her arm. "Ow!

"Help me, Mercy," Angela demanded.

Together they carefully lifted Zena from the seat of the van to the seat of the wheelchair without a baby falling out.

A nurse came running out of the hospital followed by Ryann.

"How are we doing?" she asked.

"I'm squeezing my legs together so I can at least get inside the building."

The nurse grabbed the wheelchair handles and began running toward the front door with all six of the other ladies running behind her. She then ran over a crack in the sidewalk that jolted Zena almost out of the wheelchair.

"Oh!" Zena said.

"Sorry," said the nurse.

"That's okay. I know how this all works. My friends and I could have delivered this baby in the van if I wanted to."

When Ryann and Angela looked at her with questions all over their faces, Zena added, "I'm just kidding. I didn't really want to. It would have made a mess," she winked.

"I'm feeling a little woozy," Paige said as she stopped running with the group. "I think it was Mack's driving. I just need to sit down for a minute."

Mackenzie scowled at Paige as she ran past.

Paige waved her away. "I'll be okay."

"I'll stay with you," Kayleigh said, leading Paige to a waiting room. "We'll catch up to you ladies in a few minutes," Zena heard her call.

"Don't be long. This baby is coming!" Zena called back.

Mackenzie

At first, the nurses weren't all that thrilled about all of the ladies being in the delivery room.

"Oh, they're fine. I have six other kids at home. This baby is going to be rubbed raw and exposed to germs anyway."

Mackenzie smiled at her friend's spunk. She wished she could be more like Zena, or Betty Crocker, or Martha Stewart, whatever she was in the mood to call Zena on any given day.

"Help me get up here," Zena said as she tried to get up on the table.

Mackenzie quickly moved to help. She grabbed one of Zena's legs and swung it up onto the table. That's when she noticed all the scars.

"What did you do to your legs?" Mackenzie wondered.

Zena didn't answer until she had settled back on the bed. "I was a klutzy child."

That was all she was able to say before another contraction took her breath away.

Zena's legs were forgotten as she hollered for a doctor and delivered baby number seven.

Kayleigh

"You okay?" Kayleigh asked Paige, both were still sitting out in the waiting room.

"I'll be fine."

Kayleigh handed her a cup of water.

Paige nodded. "I'll be fine," she repeated. "I just got a picture in my head when Zena said we could have helped her deliver in the van." She grimaced. "It wasn't a pleasant picture. I guess I wasn't cut out to be a doctor. And probably not a mother, either."

Kayleigh smiled at her friend. She was more than grateful for the distraction. If the truth were told, she really didn't have any desire to witness childbirth either.

A ringing cell phone made both of them reach for their purses. Kayleigh smiled and held hers up. "It's me." She walked a few paces away from Paige before she answered. "Hi, honey."

"Where are you?" her husband growled. "I thought you'd be home by now."

Kayleigh looked at her watch, not knowing what time it was. She made a face. "I'm sorry. Zena went into labor while we were at lunch. We all drove her to the hospital."

"You need to come home."

Kayleigh could tell he was angry. "Well, I'll be a little longer. My car is still at the restaurant."

"That was a stupid move. I expect dinner on the table at the same time as usual every night," he hollered before he hung up the phone.

Kayleigh disconnected from her end. She stood silently for a moment. She turned when she remembered Paige was nearby and had probably heard the entire conversation or at least got the gist of it. Thoughts of Paige made Kayleigh realize eyes were boring into her back. When she finally turned around, there were no doubts what was on Paige's mind.

Paige

"I think you should leave him," Paige said as she looked to her friend. It pained her greatly to see how Jeff treated his wife. He had never laid a hand on Kayleigh, at least not that Paige had seen, although it wouldn't have surprised her. Paige had witnessed more than once his words cut Kayleigh to the bone.

Kayleigh sighed. "I know how you feel; I know how you all feel. And by now you should know how I feel."

Paige remembered an earlier conversation they'd had on the same subject. Kayleigh had told them that when she married Jeff, she not only made a commitment to him but also to God.

Kayleigh went to look out the window. "He wasn't always like he is now. We were friends in high school and attended the same church. We went on mission's trips together. I remember the night he decided to give his life completely over to the Lord. It wasn't too long after graduation that we started dating. It was kind of a whirlwind romance."

She paused. Paige waited.

"I know he knows the Lord. I have to have faith in that."

Another pause.

"But I don't know what made him change into what he's become now."

"Maybe he only changed long enough to get you."

Kayleigh didn't reply to that.

"I think it's ironic how he's a psychologist who says he can help people when he can't even help himself or treat you right." As soon as the words were out of Paige's mouth, she knew they were the wrong words. Especially when Kayleigh turned around to glare at her. She grimaced at herself and balled her hands into fists. When would she ever learn what not to say?

Deciding not to push the issue when she could tell Kayleigh was upset, Paige decided to change the subject. "Do you think there's a new baby up there yet?"

"There's only one way to find out." Kayleigh gave Paige a smile. "You feeling up to it?"

Paige nodded her head and stood up. She pretended not to notice the tear she saw in Kayleigh's eyes and clamped her lips shut for fear of yet another misspeaking mishap.

Angela

Angela stood back from the rest of the group as they ooo'd and aaahhh'd over the baby. Angela found herself a little jealous of Zena. She wasn't so much jealous of Zena herself, but of what Zena had that Angela didn't.

Zena had a great husband.

Angela didn't.

Zena had six, no seven now, beautiful children.

Angela didn't and would never have any children.

When she was thirteen years old, her mother knew there was some kind of female issue. When she didn't start her period by the time she was sixteen, the doctor said she would never be able to have children. Angela believed her parents were more upset about that than she was. Even at a young age, Angela knew there were plenty of children out in the world she could adopt. But, she didn't want to do it without a husband. And after all this time Angela figured no one wanted her. It was almost too late for her to begin a family, even though it was something she desperately wanted. God didn't seem to be answering her prayers in that regard. Maybe she should get Kayleigh working on that...if she could find the courage to confide in her.

In her corner of the room, Angela privately reminisced about "the good old days." When she was in school had a crush on one boy after another. After a cry-fest with her mom one day because none of those boys liked her, her mother had given her some of the best advice ever. Angela could still hear her mom's voice.

Give every part of your life over to God. If He wants you to get married, He will send along the right boy at the right time. If He doesn't want you to get married, He will make you content in even that.

While Angela had handed over her love life, or lack thereof, to God she still wasn't completely sure about the contentment issue. For the most part, she accepted it, but there were moments like these that it still stung a little. On the other hand, Angela knew her singleness had allowed her to do some things a married woman wouldn't have had the freedom to do; that and the sizable inheritance she had received from her parents when they had died in an accident during her college years. Wisely invested, her money had done a lot of good for many missionaries around the world.

If Angela was honest with herself, she had to admit she used the Internet and social media to her advantage. She had looked up several of those boys she'd had crushes on. Not being married to them had been a blessing. Many of them ended up being fat, ugly, or losers. Angela knew appearance wasn't everything, but she did want to be physically attracted to her husband.

Angela had made the mistake of confiding in Paige one day about all her old crushes. That was what got Paige started on setting up Angela on blind dates. Paige felt she was a better judge of character than Angela was; however, after several of those dates Angela was not convinced of that.

"Is there a baby in here?" Paige and Kayleigh came into the room bringing Angela back to the moment.

Angela thought Kayleigh looked as if she'd been crying, but this was a happy occasion, not one to discuss difficult times…or difficult husbands, Angela figured. She'd seen that look on Kayleigh before.

"There sure is," Ryann whispered in response to their entry.

"Where's my husband?" Zena wondered.

"Don't worry," Angela said. "I already called him, and he's on his way. When he gets here, I'll take everyone back to the restaurant to get their cars and leave you three alone."

"What about the kids?"

"Aunt Angela's got that covered too. And dinner as well. The neighbor is with them now. I'm going to pick up pizza and relieve her ASAP. Speaking of which…" Mercedes was standing next to Angela. She had her arms crossed in front of her allowing Angela to see her watch. Angela grabbed Mercedes' wrist. "What time is it? Oh, I love that watch!"

"Thanks. I'll leave it to you when I die."

"I'm going to have to leave soon."

"We all came together, so we will all have to leave together." She looked to Zena and added, "In your van."

Zena just waved her hand at the group. "I'm not going anywhere."

"I'll drive." Angela grabbed the keys away from Mackenzie.

"What?" Mackenzie acted as if she were offended.

Angela made a face. "You know what."

Ryann

Ryann could not stop smiling as she watched Zena hold her baby for the first time. Ryann had forgotten how tiny babies were.

"I need to give you some extra instructions for when you go home." The doctor was talking to Zena.

Zena interrupted him with a wave of her hand. "I don't know what you would tell me that I don't already know, but tell Ryann. I'm too out of it to remember anything you say. My husband isn't here yet, and she's the next best thing."

"Who's Ryann," he asked looking around at each of them.

Ryann raised her hand.

The doctor began to speak, giving basic instructions that any mother of seven would know. Suddenly, he stopped talking.

"Are you all right?" he asked Ryann. He looked deep into her eyes.

Ryann took a step back. She ran her tongue across her teeth wondering if there were some remains of her lunch there. *Perhaps I should've left the garlic bread alone at the restaurant*, she thought to herself.

As he looked even deeper into her eyes, if that were possible, she began to wonder if he was flirting with her. It had been so long since her flirting days, she wasn't quite sure what that looked like anymore.

"Are you okay?" he asked again. "Your eyes…" He didn't finish his statement.

"I'm fine. Zena is the one who probably needs you right now." She nodded her head in Zena's direction.

Before he turned to attend to Zena, he handed Ryann a business card. "Call me. Soon."

Kayleigh

Kayleigh tried to stay back in the shadows of the hospital room. Yes, she was very happy for Zena, but Kayleigh's husband had put a damper on her ability to celebrate.

When Zena's husband came in, he acted like this was their first baby instead of their seventh. He gushed over the baby so much so that it made Kayleigh almost sick to her stomach. When he gave Zena a tender, yet passionate kiss, it almost did Kayleigh in.

When Kayleigh was a little girl, she dreamed of a husband who would love her. She dreamed of living happily ever after. However, it wasn't too long into her marriage when she realized fairy tales were fiction.

Except of course for Zena and her husband.

Is it too much to ask, God? Why can't I have that? Kayleigh sent up a quick complaint. Then, just as quickly she sent up an earnest prayer. *I put Jeff and my marriage in your hands, Lord. I pray that someday he will come to know You and be the husband I need him to be.*

Ryann

Later that evening as Ryann readied herself for bed, she took a good long look at herself in the mirror. She looked deep into her own eyes but saw nothing out of the ordinary. What the doctor had said to her at the hospital earlier that day had left her a little ruffled. What had he seen that concerned him? Was it even concern at all, or something else completely?

If the doctor's comment wasn't enough, when she picked up her Bible before bed, the Scriptures unnerved her as well. She read Matthew 6 and verse 22 stood out to her. "The eye is the lamp of the body. If your eyes are healthy, your whole body will be full of light."

Was God trying to tell her Mercedes was right that she needed to go to the doctor's again to get another opinion of her health? Did she need to really listen this time and not hear only what she wanted to?

Ryann got out of bed and quietly snuck down to the kitchen where she had plopped her purse. She rummaged through it looking for the doctor's business card she had stuck in there thinking to throw it away later. But now she pulled it out and stared at it. Dr. Sean Bostic. Why would an obstetrician be so adamant she called him? She rolled her eyes and tossed the card on the table. She chided herself. It was probably an elaborate come on. It has been some time since that happened, and she wasn't in the least bit interested.

As she turned to go back to bed something stirred within her. While Ryann couldn't explain exactly what it was, there was no doubting she felt it. Heard it.

Call him.

This was strange. Ryann had never felt anything like it before. She stopped, listened, and felt/heard it again.

Call him.

The only thing she knew to do was to ask her friends to pray. When she returned to her bedroom she pulled up the group text on her cell phone and sent out a quick request to pray. Ryann didn't feel it necessary to give any details. While there were times she gave specifics, there were many more times she kept the details to herself. When she did that it allowed her more readily see God's work in her life. She loved that.

Almost immediately after she hit the send button, responses started coming in. Ryann was finally able to fall asleep knowing her closest friends were lifting her up in prayer before the Throne of Grace even while she slept.

She did sleep soundly, but when she awoke her first thought was of the doctor and his business card that still sat on her kitchen table. The urge to call was just as strong, if not stronger than it had been the evening before. It was still early, but Ryann figured she could call and leave a message and not think about it anymore. She was quite surprised when someone actually answered. Ryann stumbled over her words because of that surprise. Eventually, she was able to get out her name and who she was.

"Of course I remember you. I already spoke to a colleague of mine, and we would like to meet with you for a consultation."

"Oh." Again, Ryann didn't know what to say.

"I'm sure it sounds a little strange, but I assure you it's legitimate. Also, there's no fee for the consultation if that's something you are worried about."

That was the least of her concerns.

"No," was all she said.

"Just come in for the first consultation. If you don't want anything to do with us after that it's not a problem."

Go.

There was that hear/feel thing again.

"When?"

"We can get you in first thing this morning." Then the doctor rattled off an address.

Ryann was happy to hear it was a doctor's office group she was familiar with. That eased her reservations some.

"I'll be there."

When she hung up she realized she had barely enough time to get herself ready. Scrambling to get there on time, she called her boss on the way to let him know she might be a few minutes late. It wasn't long before she was ushered into a rather plush office.

"Come on in."

Ryann felt somewhat at ease with their welcoming smiles and the open door office atmosphere. If Mercedes had known what Ryann was planning, she would have spoken to her as if she was a child and then would have demanded to go with her. For some reason, Ryann felt this was something she needed to do alone.

"Ryann, this is my colleague Dr. Bernard. Obviously, from my business card, you can see that I work in obstetrics; Dr. Bernard works in oncology, but we also work together in other ways."

The "O" word was a word Ryann hated to hear almost as much as the "C" word.

"We are believers in Christ, and while we are both qualified in our fields as far as our education is concerned, we still look to The Great Physician for help. It is He who heals and makes us successful in everything we do."

Ryann liked the sound of that. She depended on God for strength in her day-to-day life. It was comforting to know these men did as well.

"I want to examine your eyes," Dr. Bernard said as he walked closer to her.

Now Ryann was a little confused. "But my eyes are fine."

"The eye is the lamp of the body..."

Ryann's eyes opened wide when he quoted the same verse she had read just last night.

"We believe God allows us to see what we need to see when taking a closer look at your eyes," Dr. Bostic explained.

Now Ryann was beginning to wonder about their credibility. This was something she had never heard of before. However, she sat still as Dr. Bostic examined her left eye, her right eye, and back to the left again.

"I'm a little concerned about something I see in your left eye. That's what Dr. Bostic saw in the hospital yesterday that alerted him to the fact you might have an issue. I would really like you to have a mammogram very soon. I think you may have cancer in your left breast."

Ryann was shocked. She didn't respond as she was unsure of what to say. This was all so surreal, almost unbelievable.

"I know what you're thinking," Dr. Bernard broke into her thoughts. "That I can't be for real. Make an appointment with your regular doctor and get a mammogram. I would like to know the results, but I'm not going to badger you."

A little while later when Ryann left the doctor's office, she still didn't know what to think. She hadn't had a mammogram in a while and knew her insurance would pay for it. She felt a sudden urgency to call her doctor and make an appointment. Right after she called her doctor, she called Mercedes.

"I'll go with you," was Mercedes' reply to Ryann's story.

Mackenzie

After she had put the boys to bed for the night, Mackenzie sat down and had a good cry. She couldn't believe what had happened. She didn't need one more thing on her plate. She had always known life was not fair, but the phone message she came home to was the icing on the cake. She leaned forward with her elbows on her knees and put her head in her hands.

"I can't handle this right now, God," were the only words she could think of to say. Then something someone had told her long ago came to her mind. *God will never give you more than you can handle.* Mackenzie couldn't help but snort. "I think You've overestimated my strength, Lord."

When she wasn't praying, all she could hear was her mother's voice reverberating in her head.

"You should never have married 'what's his name'!"

"I told you not to leave home."

There were a hundred other phrases her mom would spout off to remind Mackenzie of all her mistakes in life. That was part of the reason she had left home in the first place, and they certainly weren't going to bring her back now.

Then she responded to another voice that was calling to her. It was the pint of Rocky Road ice cream she knew was in the freezer. She grabbed the container and went to bed to cry and wallow in her self-pity a little bit more. So much for her diet.

Chapter 3

The only way to have a friend is to be one. - Ralph Waldo Emerson

November

Angela

Call Mackenzie.

Angela looked up from the floor she was mopping and stood perfectly still. She noticed it again.

Call Mackenzie.

Angela did not even wait until she had finished her mopping. In fact, she immediately dropped the mop on the floor and grabbed her cell phone off the table.

"Hello?"

"Hey, Mack. It's Angela. How are you?"

"Fine."

But she wasn't. Angela could hear that much. "Do you want me to pick you up for lunch today or are you going to walk with Mercy?"

"Oh, is today lunch day?"

Angela didn't think Mackenzie was very good at pretending. Angela wasn't sure what was going on, but she played along, hoping to get some information. "Yes, same day as last month and the month before that, and the month before that."

"I forgot it was today. Maybe I'll just skip this month."

"You can't. We all need to be there or it won't seem right," Angela tried to change Mackenzie's mind.

"I don't know..." Mackenzie began.

Angela wasn't sure, but she had an idea of what the problem might be. "I forgot. I have a gift card to the restaurant, and I was going to give it to you. I'll make sure I stick it in my purse before I leave to pick you up." And just so Mackenzie couldn't argue any further, Angela added, "I'll see you in an hour." Then she ended the call.

After that, Angela hurried to get ready to go. She needed to allow herself a few extra minutes to stop at the store and grab a gift card.

Angela had wondered about Mackenzie's financial situation for a while, but she'd never had any definitive proof of anything. There were just little signs, probably nothing most people would pick up on. But Angela was not most people.

First, there was Mack only ordering water at lunch. At the time Angela had kind of chalked that up to Mackenzie trying to be a little healthier and lose some weight. But then Angela noticed Mackenzie would often order just a side salad or an appetizer and call it lunch. Even then Angela didn't put all the pieces to the puzzle together until she saw Mackenzie counting out change to pay her lunch bill. That day, Angela also noticed Mack left hardly anything for a tip. Angela left a larger than necessary tip with her payment.

The phone call with Mack today was another dot. Separately, they didn't seem to mean much but once connected, Angela could see the bigger picture.

"Lord, allow me to see where I can best be a help to Mackenzie. I know it's hard for her raising those two boys by herself without help from anyone. I don't know if there's something she's hiding from us, but she has no secrets from You. Help me be a blessing to her in whatever way You know is best. Amen."

Mackenzie

Mackenzie was not particularly happy with Angela. Yes, Mackenzie had lied about remembering lunch day, but she wanted to stay at home and continue to wallow in her pity. She didn't feel like getting dressed and making herself presentable for the public. She hadn't even showered in a couple of days. She was beginning to smell bad, even to herself.

She wasn't sure how the boys had managed without her attention. She had just gone through the motions of preparing meals...she had prepared them meals, right? Well, there were a lot of dirty dishes piling up in the sink if that was any indication. Shaking her head, Mackenzie gathered a towel and clean clothes. Maybe a shower wasn't a bad idea. Angela wasn't going to take no for an answer. She said she was going to be there in an hour, and she would be there in an hour. Angela was punctual if nothing else. Mackenzie needed to get moving. She took Cameron to Mrs. Schuyler next door and then made herself presentable. Mrs. Schuyler was used to seeing Mackenzie not dressed or showered.

Once she was ready, Mackenzie kept looking out the front window. When Angela pulled her car up to the house, Mackenzie grabbed her coat and went out to meet her. It wouldn't help the situation any to allow Angela to see the state of the house. Angela would have a solution for that as well. The go-getter would probably organize a cleaning party immediately following lunch, and then there would be a counseling session until Mackenzie spilled the beans.

As soon as Angela pulled up, Mackenzie all but ran out the door promising herself she would clean later that afternoon and bring her focus back to being a better mom.

"Hello!" She tried to put on a happy face and sound as cheerful as possible.

"Hello!" Angela said, a little over the top.

Inwardly Mackenzie cringed. Angela had purposely matched her not so sincere emotions. She would have to be more careful. These women knew her well and it wouldn't take long before they were on to her. If they thought there

50

was something wrong, they would all but sit on her until she told them what was bothering her. It was like having six nosey, big sisters. Some days she loved that. Other days not so much. Today she was feeling the not so much attitude.

"Anything new going on in your life?"

Mackenzie knew this was Angela's way of trying to find information. Mackenzie wasn't ready to give it.

"Nope. Same old, same old."

Angela shrugged her shoulders. "I guess no excitement is good, right?"

Mackenzie couldn't argue with that. "That's true." She nodded her head.

An awkward silence filled the car for a couple of minutes.

"Is there something you want to talk about?" Angela asked.

"Nope."

After another awkward pause, Angela added, "You know you can talk to me about anything, don't you?"

"Yup."

Mackenzie looked out her window so she could discreetly wipe away a tear. Then she busied herself with her purse and getting out of the car as soon as Angela parked. A deep breath of fresh air was necessary for her to be able to face her friends. At least none of the others seemed to be on to her as Angela was.

Zena

Zena walked into the restaurant with a huge smile on her face and a considerably smaller physique than last month. She saw Mackenzie and Angela waiting for everyone else.

"You look great!" Angela smiled and gave Zena a hug.

"You didn't bring the baby with you?" Mackenzie added with a pout on her face.

Zena shook her head. "Nope. This is my first time in the month since she's been born that I have been away from her."

"I hope you enjoy your free time," Angela said as they all sat down.

Soon everyone else arrived. Paige was the last one, as usual.

"Hey, where's the baby? I wanted to get my hands on her and her sweet cheeks," Paige said as she sat down next to Zena.

"Cooper is watching her. He said I needed a lunch date with friends."

"Must be nice." Paige had a way of saying things that sometimes hurt.

Zena knew Paige well enough to know she probably didn't mean to sound the way she did. Still, Paige's comment upset her. Perhaps it was a touch of the postpartum blues. Ignoring the chatter from the other ladies around her, Zena tried to compose herself, but for all her trying she could not stop the flow of tears.

"Zena," Ryann, who was sitting on the other side of her, asked. "What's wrong?"

Suddenly, all eyes were on her, something she was not fond of.

"I don't know!" she blurted out.

"It was me, wasn't it?" Paige asked. "I try to change my tone of voice, but I'm so bad at it. Sorry."

Zena grabbed Paige's hand. She was having trouble speaking. Finally, she was able to take a deep breath and speak.

First, she looked Paige. "It's not your fault. I think I'm just a little oversensitive. But it did bring back some memories, some of them not so good."

"I just meant that your life seems so perfect and it must be wonderful to have a husband who loves you so much."

Zena wiped her eyes as a couple of new tears slipped out. She shook her head before she spoke. "It wasn't always this way."

Zena mentally debated whether or not she should share her story with the women. But they were her friends, and she had said too much to backtrack now.

"My life wasn't always so perfect. Cooper is not my first husband. He's my second." Zena let that little tidbit of information sink in before saying more. She wasn't quite sure who it was, but someone definitely had a sharp intake of breath.

"I was miserable. In Greece, my parents arranged a marriage for me when I was only sixteen. He was not a good man, and I fought with my parents about it, but there was no changing their minds. Soon after we were married I found out what type of man he really was. If I ever did anything wrong, he beat me."

There were gasps from the others, but Zena didn't dare look them in the eye for fear she would lose her nerve. She just looked down at the napkin in her lap she was twisting to shreds.

"More than once he beat me so bad I almost died. He stabbed me. He burned me. And I have scars to prove it."

Hesitantly she pulled up her sleeves to reveal many of her scars. Again there were murmurs from her friends.

"Your legs?" Mackenzie asked her.

Zena nodded her head. "I have struggled all these years here in the United States to forget about them and get over my past, but the scars are a constant reminder. That is probably the reason I need to make sure my life is so ordered now. I need order.

"Since my first husband was such a bad person, I knew I had to bide my time. If I tried to escape, I knew he would come after me, find me, and probably give me one punch too many. He was involved in something terrible with terrible men. I just didn't know what. Then one night he didn't come home. Word got to me that he had been murdered. I must have subconsciously been planning for a long time, because I immediately packed my bags, grabbed my passport and the money he kept at the house, and ran as far as I could. To another country."

"What about your parents?" Ryann asked.

Zena shrugged. "They were the ones who forced me into that situation to begin with. I knew there had to have been money involved. If they knew I no longer had a husband they probably would've done the same thing to me again. I didn't wait around long enough to find out."

"Well, we are glad you're here now," Mercedes said.

"And safe," Angela added.

Now Zena dared to look up at her friends. They were all using their napkins to wipe their own tears. She noticed Kayleigh had sunglasses on but chose not to comment at that moment. Now was not the time, even though she knew Kayleigh had scars of her own. She could see them in Kayleigh's eyes.

"Now, let's not waste the time we have together today. Please, let's enjoy our lunch. That is my past, and this is my present." Zena smiled at them all. "God has been so good to me. He blessed me with a new husband who loves me. I have seven healthy children. I have all of you." She grabbed the hands of the ladies who sat on either side of her. "What more could I ask for?"

Paige

"Zena's spilling her guts, Paige. What's so important that you have to keep checking your phone?"

Paige quickly looked up to Mercedes. "I have someone coming to repair my windshield. They had an opening today and said they would do it while I was here since I already had plans. Can't skip lunch day, ya know!"

"What happened to your windshield?" Mackenzie wondered.

"I was driving down the highway behind a truck full of tires. The truck hit a pothole hard enough to disengage the latch on the tailgate sending tires bouncing and rolling everywhere, including one that cracked my windshield."

She spoke as though it was a fairly common occurrence. Paige was no stranger to unusual happenings. It took Paige a few moments to realize no one was talking as she looked down at her phone texting the repair man. When she did finally look up, she noticed everyone was staring at her.

Ryann shook her head and broke the silence. "Only you, Paige, only you."

Kayleigh

All the attention at the table suddenly turned to Kayleigh when Paige set her phone down, look up, and blurted out, "What's the deal with the sunglasses, Kayleigh?"

Kayleigh suddenly inhaled, partly from Paige's question being overly loud and partly simply from Paige's question.

Leave it to Paige to take notice and be loud about it, Kayleigh thought to herself. Outwardly, she smiled and lied. "I had an eye exam this morning and the doctor had to dilate my eyes."

"Oh, I hate having that done," Mercedes said.

"Me too," Kayleigh agreed. "He said I should be able to see in a while, and I should be able to work the rest of the day."

"My eye doctor told me that too. He lied," Ryann commented. "I couldn't see a thing. It was all I could do to drive myself safely home and get to bed. Now, I schedule it on my day off and get someone to drive me."

"I'll have to remember that next time." Kayleigh felt bad about lying to her friends, but she didn't know what else to do. She looked up to see Zena staring at her with a strange expression on her face. It was almost as if she could see deep down into Kayleigh's soul. Kayleigh found it quite unnerving.

She can't know, can she? Kayleigh had chosen her sunglasses particularly because the sides wrapped around her face. It would be very difficult for anyone to see what she was hiding, even for anyone sitting right next to her.

She glanced over to see Paige staring at her as well.

Kayleigh pasted on a smile for the benefit of Zena and Paige and any other of the ladies who felt the need to stare at her.

Great! Now I'm paranoid!

Ryann

Ryann didn't know what was really going on with Kayleigh. Ryann knew Kayleigh had a scoundrel for a husband. That was no secret. And while she had noticed Paige and Zena looking strangely at Kayleigh, Ryann was too absorbed in her own problems to give it much thought.

"Speaking of doctors' appointments..." Mercedes had leaned in close enough for only Ryann to hear.

At least she was a whole lot more discrete than Paige was.

Ryann smiled and reached for a breadstick so she could keep the discretion going. "I have an appointment next week."

"What day?" Mercedes asked between bites.

"Tuesday."

"What time?"

Ryann didn't answer right away; she just dropped her hand and looked to Mercedes. "Playing Twenty Questions, Mercy?"

Mercedes smiled in response.

"Nine AM," Ryann told her.

"I'll drive."

"You don't have to come with me, it's just a mammogram. What if my problem ends up being something silly, like acid reflux?"

Mercedes shrugged. "Then we'll go get some antacids together afterward."

Ryann knew there was no arguing with Mercedes.

Mercedes

Mercedes certainly did not want to jump to conclusions, but Ryann had many symptoms that were familiar. And lately, they had been fresh on Mercedes' mind. The two had been best friends for many years, and Mercedes needed to make sure Ryann was truly okay.

Annie suddenly popped into Mercedes' head. Annette, or Annie, as she was more often called by family and friends, was often the topic of Mercedes' prayers lately. The decisions Annie was making recently were not wise. However, Mercedes was trying not to be judgmental. She knew a thing or two about judgmental people and how it felt when those people shared their opinions of what was going on in one's life. Mercedes had had her fill of judgmental people long ago, yet she wasn't resentful, she was grateful. In a way, they had helped shape her into the person she was today. In fact, it was those people who helped her live up to the meaning behind her name. She always tried to be merciful and give people the benefit of the doubt.

When Mercedes found out she was pregnant with Annie, she was unmarried. In spite of the fact that she was only fifteen, people all around her asked if she was going to "rectify the situation," which meant, "Are you going to marry the father and make it right?" Like that would change what she had already done. People encouraged her to marry Evan simply because he was the father of her child. Mercedes knew it took much more than a shared baby to make a marriage work.

Even though Mercedes was unsaved at the time, she knew what she had done had crossed some moral boundary. She also knew she never truly loved Evan and had no intention of marrying him.

57

Mercedes could always feel the condescending comments as people looked down their noses at her as if they had never done anything wrong in their own lives. She knew that was a bunch of bologna.

There was one voice of reason among the others that were screaming at her, telling her what they thought she should do. That was her best friend, Ryann. Ryann had grown up in a Christian home and told Mercedes she could not correct one mistake by making another. Mercedes understood her friend was in no way insinuating her baby was a mistake. It was the choice to sleep with her boyfriend that was the mistake. It was the choice to trust birth control that was a mistake. Mercedes had taken those words to heart. She had no desire to marry Evan, which was fine with him. He quickly hit the road, and she hadn't heard from him since. She never missed him.

It had never seemed to matter to Ryann that Mercedes had become a typical, catty teenage girl. Mercedes cringed at the way she had treated Ryann those few years they had drifted apart. But Ryann, as an example of Christ, never completely shut the door on their relationship. The night Mercedes came knocking, desperate and in tears, Ryann had been there for her, just as she had been every day since

It was because of the testimony and the graciousness of her friend that Mercedes came to know the Lord.

Paige

Paige woke up smiling. It was Thanksgiving, one of her favorite days of the year. Today was one of those days she could give back in honor of those who had given so much to her over the years. There had certainly been some lean times for her and Grammy, and Paige recalled the two of them spending a Thanksgiving and even a Christmas or two or three eating dinner at a local shelter. They had no family to speak of, and when Paige was a child, they were not part of a church family. They also had no money for a big family dinner. Grammy had always played it up.

"There is no way the two of us can eat a whole turkey by ourselves. What do you say we go to this little place I know and make some new friends?"

That all sounded great to a five-year-old. It wasn't until Paige was an adult that she figured out they were going to a shelter for poor people. The extrovert in her simply enjoyed meeting new people and making new friends, especially the man she now knew as the director, Mr. Roger. He would always have some special treat for her each year she came, usually a stuffed animal. He always made her feel so special.

Now, Paige knew he spent a lot of time watching claw machines at the grocery stores. He had figured out the system and always won toys. He kept those toys in a box in his office. Each time a child came in he would get out one of those stuffed animals and give it away. He had made a lot of friends that way, and Paige was a lifelong one. She wanted to be like Mr. Roger.

The two stood side-by-side as they served everyone with a welcome smile and a warm meal.

"Well, they don't look like the norm."

Paige followed Mr. Roger's gaze to the front entrance where she saw a bunch of familiar faces.

"What are you guys doing here?"

"You're always talking about how much fun you have serving people. We thought maybe we could give up a little bit of our day to share in that." Ryann answered for the entire group.

Paige smiled and looked to Mr. Roger. "These are my friends." She pointed to each one as she introduced them. "Do you have a place to put them to work?"

Mr. Roger smiled too. "You bet. Come on back here so I can give you aprons. Then I'll assign you a spot."

Paige couldn't help but notice as the lunch ladies passed by that Zena pulled a brightly colored apron she no doubt made herself, out of her purse.

"Always prepared, aren't you?" Paige teased as Zena walked by with a wink.

Paige didn't know when she last had such an enjoyable Thanksgiving. The lunch ladies stayed and helped most of the day, and then they ended up back at Ryann's house where her girls had prepared a feast for everyone. Paige couldn't stop looking at the smiling faces of her friends. The laughter from young and old was contagious – a sound she would never tire of hearing.

She wished everything would stay the same as it was in that moment, that they would all stay the same age, the children would all maintain their innocence. Life was just about as perfect as it could be.

Chapter 4

One who has unreliable friends soon comes to ruin, but there is a friend who sticks closer than a brother. - Proverbs 18:24

December

Zena

"But, Mom, we don't want to be here with all your lady friends." Zena's oldest boy, Nicholas, whined.

"Well, you should have thought about that before that whole fiasco at co-op." Her accent came out stronger when she was upset.

"We were just having fun," son number two argued, adding, "Can we please go to Nana's house?"

"You boys don't need to worry about anything going on with my friends. You will neither see them nor be seen by them. And from your room, you won't be able to hear anything either." She grabbed a shoulder of each one and gave them a tender, but firm push towards their bedroom. "I'll let you know when, or if, you can come out."

The previous week had been the last week at the homeschool co-op before Christmas break, a break that everyone needed and had been looking forward to. Some of the boys were unsupervised for a time and did as boys do and took advantage of it. Zena was still a little sketchy on some of the details.

Zena had been in her class teaching at the time, but the story she had heard was that a bunch of them were standing around the open trunk of someone's car. Talk about sketchy! If they had been anywhere else besides a church parking lot, the police probably would've stopped just to see what they were up to. Anyway, one of the boys had fallen into the trunk and it slammed shut. She wasn't sure how that happened; neither were the boys. No one in the remaining group of boys knew where the key was, so they all had to go and look for the boy's mom who owned the car, but they couldn't find her anywhere. Zena couldn't help but wonder if they had really looked.

The group of boys went off to their next classes, forgetting all about their comrade in the trunk. At least until another mom walked by and heard banging and shouts of, "Let me out!" She had no trouble finding the owner of the car to let out said boy.

Zena rolled her eyes as she walked away from the boys' room to finish preparing for the lunch ladies.

"Yep. They're grounded for life."

Paige

"Hey, everyone," Paige said as she walked into Zena's house. "Sorry I'm late."

"You're no later than usual," Angela commented. "Thankfully, Zena had some wonderful hors d'oeuvres for us."

Every December lunch was at Zena's. Besides the fact that she enjoyed cooking, she said it was too much for her to carry the goodie baskets she prepared for all of them to a restaurant.

Behind Paige the door opened, bumping her in the tush.

"Whoops, sorry." It was Mackenzie. "I figured I would be the only one who wasn't sitting at the table yet. Cameron had a doctor's appointment, and it went a little longer than I expected."

"Come in. Come in," Zena invited as she gave both Paige and Mackenzie hugs. "You're not late at all. You're right on time," she said to Mackenzie. "You can put your things over there." She pointed and Mackenzie went to put down her purse and hang up her coat. "I'm going to use the ladies' room real quick."

"I guess that means I'm right on time too, then doesn't it?" Paige grinned at Zena after Mackenzie walked away.

"No. You are late. You are always late and have no excuse."

"I do have an excuse. It's just that no one has asked me about it yet." Paige pretended to feel hurt. In reality, she just wanted to share her ridiculous story.

"What's your story?" Zena went along with the act.

"There was an accident with a chicken truck. It was on its side and there were chickens running amuck all over the road. There were a couple of farmers, I'm assuming the drivers, that were chasing them and trying to corral them. Have you ever watched someone chase a chicken? I had to help catch the chickens. I couldn't leave them out there in the road to get run over by cars."

"I feel a joke coming on," Mercedes said dryly.

"Why did the chicken cross the road?" Kayleigh giggled.

Paige stopped talking when she got the feeling no one believed her. They never did, even though every word was true.

Paige ended her story with, "I couldn't just run them over."

Mackenzie came back into the room and asked, "By the way, Paige, why are there feathers all over your car?"

Paige turned and looked directly at Zena. Her expression daring Zena to doubt her.

"Now that we're done with that..." Zena turned around and walked away.

Paige glared as Zena walked back to the kitchen wiping her hands on her apron. Paige turned around and stepped aside to get out of Mackenzie's way.

"Look at you." Paige couldn't help but shout when she actually took the time to notice Mackenzie. "You must be working hard! I can tell you've lost weight!"

Immediately Mackenzie's face changed.

Oh no, Paige wondered to herself. *Did I say the wrong thing again?*

Mackenzie just said, "Thanks," but it was clipped as if this was not a conversation she wanted to be having.

"Well," Paige began, actually considering her words before they came out of her mouth for a change. "You look great!"

Mackenzie smiled, but it was a strange smile. It seemed tired.

Angela

Even before everyone could sit down, Angela made her yearly announcement. "Next month everybody's lunch is on me."

"You don't have to pay for all of us. That's a lot of money," Mercedes said.

Angela just looked at her. "Did you hear the part about not arguing? This is my Christmas present to you all. I'm certainly not going to give you a crafty gift like Mack or basket of goodies from the fruits of my labor like Martha Stewart over there. This is something I can do and something I enjoy doing. So, just accept the gift and eat. Merry Christmas."

A chorus of thank yous and Merry Christmases filled the room.

Angela often wished she had more talent than money. Money for lunch was nice, but it wasn't personal. She smiled as she opened the homemade card from Mackenzie. Then she inwardly groaned as she looked through the goodie basket from Zena knowing more exercise would be required if she ate all of it. Zena had outdone herself. There was hot pepper jelly, elderberry jam, canned peaches, apple pie filling (which Angela knew she would eat right out of the jar since she couldn't bake anything, even a supposedly simple apple crisp), bread, cookies, fudge, vegetable soup, chicken soup, all from the bounty of Zena's farm. Everything was clearly marked and beautifully decorated with Zena-designed labels. It truly was a gift that exemplified Zena.

Mercedes

Mercedes was enjoying everything about the day. The conversation. The food. The spirit of Christmas in the air. The time spent with her best friends.

A slight vibration in her pocket stole her attention. She excused herself from the table when she glanced down and saw Annie's name pop up. Sneaking into the bathroom and closing the door, she pulled out her phone fully so she could read the entire message.

Merry Christmas, Great Grandma!

Surely that couldn't be true. She had become a mother at fifteen a grandmother at thirty, and now a great-grandmother at forty-five. She couldn't help but wonder when the cycle would end. She discreetly settled herself back at the table.

Kayleigh

"Mack, these cards are great," Kayleigh exclaimed.

Mackenzie waved it off like it was nothing. "I'm sorry. Money is a little tight this year."

Kayleigh shook her head. "Mack, this is something I will treasure forever." She held the card to her chest as the rest of the ladies agreed.

"In fact," Kayleigh continued, "I think you should try to sell them."

"I think you should have us all over and teach us how to make them," Zena said.

"I think that's a great idea!" Angela chimed in.

"Me too," Paige said as she gave her card another loving look.

"I don't know…" Mackenzie began.

"Oh, you have to," Zena said. "I want to do this for my family as part of their Christmas gifts." Zena was always thinking and planning ahead. "Wouldn't something like this look pretty tucked into a basket of food?"

Angela

Angela watched Mackenzie's face as the others begged her to teach them how to make cards. Normally, Mackenzie took every opportunity she could to teach something new.

"We can pay you to teach us," Angela added to the conversation, seeing an opportunity to help Mackenzie. She looked around at the rest of the women to see their reactions. Not one balked.

"Oh, no. I couldn't charge my friends," Mackenzie argued.

"Well then, we'll give you money to go toward buying supplies. I don't know where to get them or what to buy. Sound good, everyone?"

Angela already knew everyone else was on board, but she smiled as they agreed anyway.

"Let's do it next week so we can have some to give out before Christmas," Paige suggested.

"Great idea," Kayleigh agreed.

"Everyone bring twenty dollars to give to Mack," Angela ordered.

"That's too much," Mackenzie tried to argue.

"Buy extra so we can make lots of cards," Angela forcefully pushed a fifty dollar bill into Mackenzie's hand.

Angela watched as Mackenzie's demeanor changed, knowing she was defeated. She sighed before she said, "My place, next Thursday night at seven."

"Great! We'll all bring snacks!" offered Paige.

66

Angela smiled and looked to Ryann, who had been suspiciously quiet the entire lunch.

Mackenzie

"Hey, Mack, how is your son doing with the herbs I gave you?"

Zena's voice pulled Mackenzie away from her lunch. She was thoroughly enjoying it and at the same time remembering to savor every bite as this was more than likely to be her only meal of the day.

She shrugged her shoulders in response to Zena's question. "I thought at first he was doing a little better, but now I'm not so sure."

"Aren't you taking him to the doctors?" Paige piped in, sounding rather judgmental.

Mackenzie got defensive. "Yes. I even talked to the doctor about the herbs Zena gave me." She thought she'd throw that in before Paige found something else to say. If she didn't love Paige so much, she'd smack her.

Then she stopped her negative thoughts. Taking a deep breath she reminded herself, *My problems are my problems. I don't need to take them out on anyone else.*

She directed her conversation toward Zena, who had asked the question. "I'm feeling a little overwhelmed by the doctor. He keeps telling me all the things it could be, but he never seems to come up with anything definitive. It breaks my heart to see Cam going through so many tests, especially the ones that cause him pain." It also broke the bank to pay for all those extra tests. She felt as if she had to call the insurance company every day about something.

"Is part of the problem because Cameron is so young?" Zena wondered. "I mean, he probably can't communicate well enough to tell you how he's feeling or what hurts or whatever."

Mackenzie thought about that a moment before responding. "That may be partly true. I know I get frustrated when he just cries and I can't help."

Zena nodded in agreement. "I've been there. I think all parents have been there at some point in their parenting journey, but it's hard when it goes on and on. My oldest was having issues when we decided to start the farm; we wanted to make sure his diet was as pure as we could possibly get it. We raise our own meat and grow our own fruits and vegetables."

"I wish I could do that," Mackenzie shook her head. "But it's not possible for me."

"I'd be glad to help anywhere I can. I can show you how to can your own food, such as soups," Zena offered.

"I'd still be buying food from the store to make those soups."

"No, you won't. Next summer when my garden is overflowing with vegetables you're going to come over and we will make some vegetable soup to start with. We'll have way more than we can eat."

Mackenzie smiled a sad smile. She loved Zena's hospitable heart, but right now, summer seemed so far away. For today, though, she would make her gift basket last as long as she possibly could.

Ryann

While the others all ate and chattered away, Ryann's mind wandered elsewhere; to her four daughters to be exact. What were they going to do? Jocelyn and Tessa were old enough to take care of themselves, but would they be able to hold down jobs, keep the house running, and take care of Riley and Maddie at the same time?

Not that she would ever admit it to anyone, not even Mercedes who knew more about her than anyone else did, but she had spent all morning researching online. She should never have done that. It psyched her out to the point that she was paranoid that she could suddenly drop dead with no warnings or anything.

It was all in God's hands now. She had to leave it there.

She looked up from her chicken Parmesan to see Mercedes and Angela staring at her.

"You're awfully quiet today. You feeling all right?" Angela asked her.

"I'm okay," Ryann answered with a forced smile, not even convincing herself. Trying to change the subject, she spoke to Zena.

"It's pretty quiet around here. Where are all the kids?"

"My saint of a mother-in-law took them to her house for the entire day, except of course for the two that are grounded. I love having my kids around all the time, but I'd be lying if I said I didn't enjoy a break every now and then."

Ryann smiled. She remembered the days when her girls were little. If only she could go back at least for a little while.

"You don't get away with it that easily."

Ryann looked up to see Mercedes boring holes into her. "Did you get the test results back?"

Ryann couldn't speak. She could only nod her head, and even that was slight. She didn't have to say a word to communicate with Mercedes about what those test results were.

Immediately, Mercedes' arms were around her. As much as Ryann fought, she couldn't hold back the flow of tears. They had been around the edges of her eyes all day.

Why did the doctor have to call today? Couldn't he have let me finish out a good year with my lunch lady friends? Now I've ruined lunch.

Ryann knew her thinking was ridiculous even as she thought the words. Of course, the doctor had no idea what her plans were for the day or how much she enjoyed this one day a month with her best friends. Even though her head was buried in Mercedes' shoulder, she knew everyone was waiting for her to tell them what was wrong.

"Do you want me to tell them?" Mercedes whispered in Ryann's ear.

Ryann nodded, thankful Mercedes had insisted on being there for her when she went to the doctors. Mercedes had heard the word cancer and had held Ryann's hand during the biopsy. Mercedes had been there for her like no one else ever had been before.

By the time Mercedes was done sharing Ryann's bad news, Ryann had managed to compose herself, at least enough to speak a little, as long as she did not look her friends in the eyes since they had come undone themselves.

"Why didn't you tell us?"

Ryann didn't mind Paige's harshness.

"We could have been praying for you," Kayleigh wiped her eyes on her napkin.

"The doctor just called with the results this morning. I wanted to wait until after Christmas to tell everyone. I didn't want to ruin anyone's holidays."

"Pish-posh," Zena said, putting her arms around Ryann. "You let us know what you need. I'll bring food."

"I'll pray every day," Kayleigh laid her hand on Ryann's arm.

"I'll take you to all of your appointments," Mercedes said in her usual forceful, motherly way.

"I'll make sure your house is clean when you come home from treatments," Paige offered.

Ryann had to laugh at her friends. "I do have daughters who can help me, you know!"

"Don't worry. We'll make sure they have jobs to do too," Mackenzie smiled, taking her turn to hug Ryann.

Ryann wiped her eyes once more. "You guys are the best. What would I do without you?"

"What would we do without you?" Paige threw the question back at her.

Mercedes

70

When the conversation reverted back to happier topics, Mercedes leaned over to Paige.

"Do you know you could benefit from self-control?" she asked.

"How?"

"You will have a better relationship with all your friends. Your friends will be more satisfied with you. You'll feel more secure in those friendships. Your friends will be more apt to forgive you when you do say the occasional stupid thing. Self-control can eliminate conflict among friends and prevent a friend from feeling rejected."

Paige just stared at Mercedes, her face all scrunched up in question.

"It's true," Mercedes said before taking a sip of her water. "I read it on the Internet. On a blog in fact. So it has to be true."

Realization finally appeared on Paige's face. "Oh. I get it."

"You really should learn to control your tongue."

"I know," Paige whispered.

"I'm not trying to be mean. Take it as just some motherly advice. People will come to resent you, and I don't want that to happen. You're a sweet girl, and I know you mean well." Mercedes put her hand on Paige's leg.

"I know," Paige repeated. "My mouth just speaks before my mind has a chance to think. Sometimes it's like I don't have any control over it."

"I know exactly what you mean. You have a gift for seeing the truth of many matters. It's your delivery that needs the work. God has blessed us all with gifts, we just sometimes need to work together to develop them. I used to be the same way."

Paige's mouth gaped. "No! I don't believe it. I'm jealous of your ability to always know the right thing to say... Or not say... Or how to say it."

Mercedes nodded her head. "It's true. In my younger days, I was known to be quite snarky."

"But how did you change?"

Mercedes bobbed her head back and forth. "There was one thing that helped me change. First of all, I found out what it was like to be on the receiving end of biting remarks, and I didn't like it. After that, I tried quitting on my own, but you know what they say, 'old habits die hard.' Then I turned to Christ. I realized He was the only One who could help me change. I handed all my bad habits over to Him."

"Just like that? You gave it to God, and it was gone?"

"Not exactly. I still had to learn to control my tongue, but at least then I had God to help, which made it a whole lot easier. It still took time to break old habits and to build new ones."

"I'll have to try that."

"I'll be praying for you," Mercedes said with a smile. What Mercedes wouldn't give to take back some of the words she had spit out when she was younger! Maybe she could help Paige not have to go down that same road. It was a bumpy one to be on.

Paige

As good as Zena's cooking was, Paige picked at her food. There was something she had wanted to say for the longest time, but she was a little nervous. She wanted to do something different but was afraid to even suggest it. She often felt like the ignored, neglected little sister being the youngest of the group. Yes, the others were older and probably wiser, but did it hurt to make a suggestion and do something new and different once in a while? She was tired of always eating lunch at the same place. Of course, there were only four things on the menu she had the nerve to try at Bistro 316. She took a deep breath before blurting out her idea, fully expecting to be shot down quickly.

"I vote we begin the New Year eating at a new restaurant," Paige burst out, regardless of the other conversations that were going on around the table. Mercedes looked at her with a did-we-not-just-discuss-this face. Paige took a deep breath, reworded the question, and softened her voice so it sounded a little less grumpy. "I mean would anyone else like to try a different restaurant next month?"

Mercedes sent her a smile and a discreet wink.

"Why would we change?" Kayleigh asked.

"Yeah. We like where we go," Angela added.

"We can't change restaurants. Bistro 316 has sentimental value. That is where Cooper and I had our first date," Zena added.

Paige rolled her eyes as she was reminded of Zena's perfect love story. As soon as Cooper saw Zena, it was love at first sight, at least for Cooper. Zena had felt too damaged to be interested in dating anyone. Besides, Cooper was a little too nerdy for Zena's taste. But, after months of persistence, Zena finally gave in to Cooper. She thought of it as a pity date and hoped he would leave her alone after one dinner. But that wasn't what happened.

Cooper fell in love with Zena even more. On their first date, here, at Bistro 316, he told her that God had created her for him. Zena allowed the relationship to go on for about two weeks, but then she broke it off with him. She had grown scared, terrified actually, of getting any closer to him. She could not surprise him on their wedding night with her scarred body, and she was in no way ready to share her story with him yet.

Even though Zena had called it quits on the relationship, Cooper didn't. He still continued to call her, stop by her apartment with flowers he had picked from some field he probably wasn't supposed to pick them from. Finally, nerdy Cooper convinced Zena to give it a go again. God had worked on Zena's heart during all that time, and He had convinced her to share her past with Cooper. She figured it might just scare him away once and for all. Cooper sat and listened with rapt attention. When Zena was done talking, he told her he would treat her like a queen for all the days of his life. And up to this point he had. Sometimes Paige thought they were utterly disgusting in their love.

Paige had vowed to herself that if she ever found someone, she would never allow it to get so sappy.

Coming back to the present conversation, Paige looked at Zena.

"Well, *we* aren't married." When she emphasized the "we" she gestured to everyone around the table.

"They always save the back room for us," Ryann added.

"That's because they don't want us disturbing the other patrons," Mercedes added her own thoughts.

Everyone laughed and agreed. They could get a little loud from time to time.

The rest of the ladies conceded, but not too enthusiastically.

"You pick the new restaurant," Mercedes said, looking at Paige.

"Oh…um…" For once Paige was at a loss for words. "How about that new Italian place on the corner near church? I've been wanting to it try ever since I started smelling their food when we leave church on Sunday afternoons."

Everyone agreed to the new lunch meeting place, again, not all that enthusiastically.

"I have a bad feeling about this," Zena said, shaking her head.

Paige ignored Zena's comment.

Angela

After lunch was over and they had all gone their separate ways, something was nagging at Angela. Yes, there was the revelation of Ryann's cancer, but there was something else as well. She mentally recalled where each one of them had sat at the table and what each one of them looked like.

When she got to her recollection of Mackenzie, she stopped. She remembered how methodical Mackenzie was while she ate. It was weird. She had taken small, slow bites and didn't leave a crumb on her plate. Mackenzie wasn't one for wasting food, but her actions were not the normal Mack at all.

On a whim, she decided to call Mackenzie to see if she needed anything. Looking at the time she decided to call Mackenzie at work. It wasn't a practice she liked, but Mack was usually the one that answered the phone anyway. Surely a quick call wouldn't hurt.

"I'm sorry, Mackenzie doesn't work here anymore," the voice on the other end said.

As much as Angela wanted to get information, she knew this woman wouldn't give her any. She then dialed the number of the only person who could give her information: Mackenzie.

When Mackenzie answered the phone, Angela decided to be a little deceptive. She figured that would be better than hurting her friend's feelings because she had obviously kept her job situation to herself.

"Oh, hey, Mack. I didn't expect you to answer the phone. I was just going to leave you a message while I had something on my mind. I assumed you would be at work."

"No, not today." Mackenzie answered quickly, almost too quickly.

Angela didn't want to push, so she made something up. "Well, I needed to finish my Christmas shopping this week, and I wondered what the boys wanted.

Yeah, that sounded legitimate, she thought to herself.

"Oh. I don't know. They like pretty much anything. They always enjoy everything you get them, but please, don't feel obligated."

"Don't be ridiculous! If I can't buy for everyone else's kids, who can I buy for?"

"Well, if I think of something specific I'll give you a call back," Mackenzie said.

"That would be great."

As much as she wanted to, Angela forced herself not to ask. Instead, she ended the call on her part with one more little push. "You have a great rest of the day off."

Okay, I tried, she told herself. Sometimes her manipulative tendencies went into overdrive. And they usually worked.

"Angela?" Apparently, Mackenzie hadn't hung up yet.

"Yes?"

"I lost my job."

"What happened," Angela asked. Mackenzie had always been a good worker as far as Angela knew.

"I was taking too many days off because of Cameron being so sick and needing to take him to all his doctor's appointments. And then there was…" Mackenzie's voice trailed off.

Angela had to wait for Mackenzie to share the rest of the story. She could tell it was hard for Mackenzie.

"And then the worst part of it was that they caught me eating food off people's plates." Mackenzie's voice got uncharacteristically loud as she laid all her shame on the table. "I didn't do it as I was taking food out to customers; I did it as I was cleaning up their leftovers. I ate their scraps so I wouldn't have to buy food for myself. I barely had enough money to buy groceries for the boys, I also knew I had to keep my own strength up so I could continue to work and take care of them."

Angela wiped tears away as one of her dearest friends laid her soul bare.

"I ate people's scraps!" Mackenzie was almost shouting. "Every time I snuck a bite into my mouth, all I could think of was that story in the Bible about the prodigal son who ate the pigs' food. Now look where that got me." Mackenzie sniffled. "I'm so ashamed and embarrassed." Her voice had retreated to its normal volume.

"Why didn't you ask us for help?" Angela wondered.

"Would you have if you were in the same situation?"

Angela didn't answer right away. She didn't have one. She knew that desperate times called for desperate measures, and Mackenzie had certainly found herself in desperate times…and with two little boys who depended on her for everything.

"Well, don't worry about groceries. I'll take care of that for you until you're back on your feet."

"Please don't tell the others. I just really needed to let it all out to someone. I don't want Jordan to know anything is wrong. Cameron is too little to notice."

"I won't say a word," Angela promised. "But don't be afraid to ask for help when you need it."

Mackenzie snorted. "I'm not sure asking for help is in my nature."

"Then look to God." That was the only other bit of advice Angela could think of.

"That I can do. I just feel overwhelmed. These last few months God has put too much on my shoulders. I can't handle anymore by myself."

"Mack, you don't have to handle it on your own. God wants you to turn to Him. He can bear the weight of all your burdens so you don't have to. Not to mention all of us. We are here for you. You just have to say the word."

"I don't deserve anyone's help."

"Why not?"

Mackenzie didn't speak at first.

"What is it?" Angela pressed.

Mackenzie took a deep breath. "Sometimes I feel as if God doesn't love me. That He's punishing me by keeping Cameron sick."

At first, Angela was completely unaware of how to respond. "I don't think God works that way. Why would He want to punish you?"

"I have no idea. I've racked my brain trying to figure it out, but I always come up empty."

Angela took a moment to think before answering. "Mack, I believe God will test us so that we do turn to Him. We can't do everything on our own. We need Him. I couldn't face one day without Him."

Mackenzie didn't respond, Angela thought she had done enough preaching and moved the topic back to Mack's loss of work.

"What are you going to do about a job?" Angela knew Mackenzie didn't have anyone else.

"I don't know. Take one day at a time, look for a job, and see what comes up."

Angela's planning mind now took a turn running in overdrive. *What can I do to fix this? Call the other ladies in the group.*

"I'm so sorry to hear this, Mack. Please let me know if there is anything I can do. I'll watch the boys if you need to fill out applications or go to interviews. I can even help babysit while you work at least some days."

"Thanks. I'm going to look for something I can do at home. If you hear of anything, please let me know."

"I will."

Angela had barely disconnected from Mack when she called the next lunch lady.

"I want to make this Christmas the best ever for Mack and the boys," she began telling everyone as she made the rounds calling the group. That was all she had to say and in turn, each lady was on board. Soon everyone was involved, and they each had assignments they would eagerly fulfill. Angela dubbed it "Operation Christmas."

Kayleigh

Scrapbooking night at Mackenzie's came up quickly. Kayleigh was really looking forward to it. She needed to be around positive people and away from the negativity that seemed to emanate from her husband's every pore. Fortunately, this was his bowling night. He would be out well past midnight, and Kayleigh would be home and in bed before he knew the difference.

She knew she should probably have told him, but not having an argument was much easier. It was the holiday season after all, and she needed to find some merry and bright. She grabbed her snack offering and went into the house.

"Hey, Mack," she called out as she entered without knocking. How she wished she felt comfortable enough in her own home to allow her friends to come and go as they pleased. Jeff would never allow that. His home was his castle. Not hers and certainly no one else's.

"In the dining room," Mackenzie hollered back.

When Kayleigh walked in she saw everyone else was already there, except for Paige of course, whom they had all decided would be late for her own funeral.

"Oh, yummy!" Mackenzie said as she took Kayleigh's plate and added it to the others on a side table. "Please, help yourself. I made peanut butter cookies, Ryann brought cupcakes, Mercy brought a veggie tray, Zena brought these scrumptious looking pizzelles, and Angela brought these."

Kayleigh noticed that instead of trying to describe Angela's contribution she just said "these." Inwardly she smiled, not wanting to hurt Angela's feelings. But she realized Angela must have caught the jab when she piped up.

"Well, we can't all be Betty Crocker."

Paige had arrived during the conversation and now added her honest opinion. "You could have just bought something."

Kayleigh could have sworn she saw some fiery darts flying from Angela's eyes in Paige's direction.

Mackenzie must have seen it too because she immediately began giving instructions on what the plan was for the evening.

Kayleigh thoroughly enjoyed herself that night. It was nice to be able to relax and let her hair down a bit. She didn't have to guard every word that came out of her mouth, even though by now it had almost become a habit.

Mackenzie's boys were part of the evening's entertainment.

"Can I make a card, too?" Jordan had shyly asked his mom.

"Is it for a special young lady in your class?" Mackenzie asked holding his face in between her hands.

"Mom!" Jordan shuffled his feet and pulled his face away from Mackenzie's hands. The sudden deep red blotches on his cheeks were answer enough.

"Of course you can," Mackenzie smiled.

"Here, Jordan. Pull up a chair next to me, and I'll protect you from your embarrassing mom." Angela scooched her chair over to make room for his.

"Me too!" Cameron obviously felt like he was being left out.

"Pull up another chair between Jordan and me." Zena moved over to make room for one more chair.

Chatter and giggles from the boys certainly boosted everyone's spirits that evening. What an amazing thing the company of a child could be!

When they were finished with their card making, Kayleigh realized she wasn't ready to go to a cold, dark home just yet.

"I'll help you clean up, Mack," she offered.

"Oh, thanks. I really appreciate that. I'm going to put the boys to bed, and then I'll be back to help."

Kayleigh smiled. "Take your time."

As she threw away the paper plates and cups, she noticed everyone had taken their snack plates home; all except Angela that is. Kayleigh made a face when she looked down at what was left, which was most of it. She had tried to be kind and eat one, but at her first bite, she just about broke a tooth. "Too bad Zena didn't leave her dessert," she mused. Of course, they had probably eaten all of that. It didn't matter; Kayleigh would have licked the plate to remove any delicious crumbs.

Once again, she looked at Angela's dessert. She then stepped on the lever to Mackenzie's garbage can and dumped in the entire plate.

Mackenzie

She knew she should hurry back out and help Kayleigh clean up, but she just relished the quiet moments after Cameron had drifted off to sleep. He had been sick again, even though he had perked up for the evening. She was more worried now than she had ever been before.

"God, why are you doing this to me? Haven't I suffered enough? Hasn't my little boy suffered enough? Do what You feel is necessary to me, but please leave Cameron be."

Later that evening, after all was cleaned up and even Kayleigh had left, Mackenzie pulled out the envelopes the ladies had given her. She thought it strange they had each handed her an envelope instead of just handing her the cash. The more she thought about it, the more she realized something else that was strange. Each one had not only handed her money in an envelope, but it seemed each one tried to hand it to her in a secretive manner as if they didn't want the other ladies to know.

Mackenzie shook her head and shrugged her shoulders. It was late, and she was over thinking something ridiculous.

Or maybe not.

The first envelope she opened had a hundred dollar bill in it. Angela had only suggested twenty. Mackenzie proceeded to open the rest of the envelopes, each containing more than twenty dollars. When she examined the pile closer, she found there were more envelopes than ladies.

She pulled out her phone and pulled up the group text.

What did you guys do?

Angela responded first with, *What are you talking about?*

Ryann must have been typing at the same time as Angela because a *Nothing* with a winking smiley face posted half a second later.

Responding to Angela, Mackenzie said, *The money!*

In turn, each lady revealed she had given more than twenty dollars. They also revealed it was not planned amongst them. No one knew what another was doing. Then they all promised they only left one envelope.

You must have been sending up some prayers, Kayleigh texted, followed by a halo emoji.

This wasn't necessary, Mackenzie texted.

No, but apparently God told us all the same thing, came from Zena.

Imagine what it would have looked like if only one of us had ignored Him! That would have been embarrassing! came from Paige.

God has truly blessed me with the best friends ever! Good night all Mackenzie ended the call on her part, but she sat there a moment longer as a series of dings signaled each lady saying good night. Mackenzie couldn't help but laugh when Paige came in last with a *Good night, John Boy.*

∞ ∞ ∞

Angela

It was very late on Christmas Eve, or very early on Christmas morning, when Angela, as quietly as possible slipped Mackenzie's spare key into the lock on the front door.

"Shush!" she demanded the gaggle of giggling ladies behind her. "Obviously none of you are used to staying out late at night and breaking into someone's house. Control yourselves!"

As soon as the words were out of her mouth she realized she shouldn't have said anything at all. It only made them giggle all the more. She did have to admit, it was fun playing Santa. She only wished she could be there to see the looks on the boys' and Mack's faces come morning.

With only a few bumps in the night, so to speak, Angela and everyone else had the presents arranged under the tree and on the couch and halfway out into the hallway. It was a sight to behold. It made Angela smile as she stepped back to admire it. She felt someone slipping an arm around her shoulder.

"It's perfect. Thanks for coming up with the idea," Kayleigh whispered.

Angela laid her head on Kayleigh's shoulder and smiled, but only for a moment before a squeal suddenly startled her.

"It looks so great!" Paige didn't exactly shout, but she didn't exactly whisper either. Then there was her handclapping, followed by the loud "Shhhhhhh!" of five other women.

The commotion was enough to bring Mackenzie out of her bedroom, a cane upheld, looking like it could do some damage to unwanted guests.

Mackenzie

"What are you guys doing here?" She still had the cane up in the air, ready to strike.

"Surprise!" Paige said in a sarcastic voice.

Ryann took the cane away from Mackenzie. "We were trying to be quiet." She gave Paige a look.

"I'm sorry I woke you," Paige said, then put her head down.

"Woke me? You scared me half to death!" She was about to say more, but then her eyes caught sight of the tree. "What's all this?" She got as close to the tree as she could, which wasn't really very close because of the pile of presents.

"We wanted the boys to have a nice Christmas," Zena said putting her arm around Mackenzie's waist.

"We were going to just sneak out, but..." Angela said, taking her turn giving Paige a look.

"I said I was sorry." Now Paige chose to whisper.

"Well, at least now I was able to see the look on your face," Angela said.

Mackenzie heard a noise behind her, and she turned to see the shining eyes of the boys. "You should be in bed."

"We heard something."

Again, everyone looked to Paige, who folded her arms across her chest in a pout.

"Look at all the presents," Jordan said with awe in his voice.

"Lots pwesents!" commented Cameron.

"Can we open them now?" Jordan asked.

Mackenzie smiled. "I know you aren't going back to sleep anytime soon."

"Can we stay and watch?" Mercedes asked quietly.

"Don't you need to get home to your own families?" Mackenzie wondered.

"Who do you think helped us with all this?" Ryann asked.

"They know where we are, and I'm sure they'd be willing to wait for us," Zena laid her hand on Mackenzie's arm.

"Why not?" Mackenzie gave in. "Find a seat..." She stopped as she looked around the small room, now crowded with gifts, and continued. "Or a comfortable place to stand."

The boys needed no further encouragement and dove for the tree.

"This one has Cameron's name on it." He handed it to his little brother and then sat and watched him open it.

This went on for over two hours as the boys opened gift after gift, laughing in delight at each one. Mackenzie wiped tears from her eyes more than once. Somehow a cup of coffee made it into her hands. Someone must have thoughtfully brewed a pot without her even knowing it. She looked around at the group of friends who were crammed into her tiny living room. *Could there be any better women?* she wondered to herself. *No, definitely not.*

Finally, the boys were done opening all their gifts and the ladies had left to celebrate with their own families. Mackenzie looked at her two boys, who were fast asleep on the floor wrapped up in the quilts Zena had made them. She thought she'd take the opportunity to catch a nap herself. It would be a long day otherwise.

Grabbing the quilt Zena had made for her and wrapping up in it, she lay down on the couch to fall asleep, but not before wondering how Zena had found time to make three quilts in such a short amount of time.

Chapter 5

Therefore encourage one another and build each other up, just as in fact you are doing. – 1 Thessalonians 5:11

January

Angela

Angela walked into the restaurant Paige had chosen for the month. While she had to admit the aromas outside the door were enticing, the décor inside the restaurant was a little less so. For a brand new establishment, it wasn't very clean. It almost looked as if the day the builders finished their work, the restaurant opened with no time for preparation. There were splotches of spackle on the floor, the walls looked like short, little Ryann had started the painting job, but quit when she could no longer reach any higher. Off to one corner of the room was a rolled up piece of carpet. Angela just shook her head and walked to where most of the ladies were already sitting.

"Hey, everybody," she called out. She sat down and joined in the conversation

After about fifteen minutes she asked, "Did you guys already order drinks?"

"Nope," Zena answered.

"We haven't even seen a waitress yet." Ryann strained her neck toward the kitchen like she was looking for someone.

Angela couldn't help but notice that Paige said nothing. She sighed and spoke loudly to a waitress who just happened to be walking by at that moment. "Excuse me, ma'am. Can we get some drinks?"

"Uh..." The waitress looked like she didn't know what a drink was. "I guess."

The ladies took turns around the table letting the waitress know what they wanted.

"I'll be back in a little bit." She seemed exceptionally shy.

"Did we say something wrong?" Kayleigh wondered.

"I don't know," Angela said, opening her eyes up as wide as they would go.

It took another fifteen minutes and another shout out from Angela to get their drinks.

Kayleigh

When they finally received their drinks, Kayleigh said, "I know we aren't drinkers, but I still would like to propose a toast. It's a New Year and I want to encourage you all to reach for your goals and your dreams."

"Here, here!" Zena said holding up her glass of sweet tea.

"Let this be a year of new beginnings and experiences," Kayleigh smiled at all of her dear friends with whom she was blessed to have another meal.

"Does that mean you're going to leave your husband this year?" Once again Paige piped in with the wrong words.

Kayleigh's blood boiled. Oh, how she wanted to smack Paige sometimes. Fortunately, she noticed her friends took care of things for her. Angela, who was sitting next to Paige, gave her a punch in the arm. Ryann, who was sitting across from Paige, must have given her a good swift kick in the shin since Paige reached under the table at the same time Angela's jab landed on her arm.

"Ow!"

"I just meant that I wanted to pray for each of you a little more this year," Kayleigh was barely able to restrain her anger.

Mackenzie

Mackenzie felt that both Paige and Kayleigh needed the attention taken off of them. "Well, you can pray that I find my dream job this year."

She hated having other people pay for her lunch, but since she hadn't been working, she didn't have money for extras. Since it was January, Angela was fulfilling her promise to pay for everyone's lunch for their Christmas present. Angela had already called Mackenzie telling her not to worry about any upcoming lunches either. She would pay for them all until Mackenzie found a job. When Mackenzie tried to argue, Angela quickly stepped in with, "Don't deny me the blessing of blessing you."

It had taken Mackenzie a little while to wrap her mind around that idea.

She had rarely been in a position to help anyone. When she was working, there was barely enough money to take care of her boys. But the more she thought about it, she realized blessing people didn't always have to take a financial form. Mackenzie looked up at Kayleigh, who was seated across from her. Kayleigh was a constant blessing to Mackenzie. There was never a day that went by that Mackenzie didn't know Kayleigh was praying for her. During some of her darkest times, she could almost feel that someone was praying for her. In those times, if she had to guess, she would have pegged that on Kayleigh. More than once Kayleigh had sent a text saying she was praying. Mackenzie wondered if Kayleigh knew how much those texts meant.

Lord, help me bless Kayleigh by praying for her more.

Mackenzie knew Kayleigh needed those prayers with all she went through with her husband.

Help me find special ways to bless each one of these ladies You have put in my life.

As if Kayleigh could hear the thoughts going through Mackenzie's head, she announced it was time for prayer requests.

Ryann

"While we are waiting to place our orders, should that waitress ever come back, let's start a prayer list," Kayleigh said, pulling out a brand new little, black book.

"Kayleigh, you can pray for me and my treatments. My new year is inadvertently focusing on my health." Ryann hated talking about herself and her problems, but she had a feeling this would be the year she would need the most prayer ever. If she couldn't ask her closest friends to pray, who could she?

"Oh," she said suddenly as she grabbed the empty hand of the waitress as she tried to speed past their table. "I think we're all ready to order if you aren't too busy." Ryann could not contain the sarcasm in her voice although she spoke with a honey-sweet smile on her face.

Reluctantly, the waitress took down their lunch requests.

When she left, Ryann rhetorically asked, "What is her problem? I feel like we're a terrible inconvenience to her."

"Maybe she needs to be added to the prayer list," Kayleigh said.

Zena

"I have something you can pray about. I've been rolling something around in my head for a few weeks now. Maybe you can pray for God's guidance, Kayleigh."

"What is that?" Kayleigh put her pen down, intertwined her fingers under her chin, and looked straight at Zena. That told Zena she was really paying attention and truly wanted to listen to what she had to say.

Zena swallowed and took a deep breath before beginning. "I want to open a battered women's shelter on our farm. I feel like I've been hiding my scars for far too long. I want other women to know they are beautiful in spite of any scars they may carry. I want them to know God loves them and that sometime down the road they might be able to help someone who's in a similar situation."

"That sounds like a wonderful idea!" Kayleigh said, picking up her pen and jotting down a note in her book.

"Your farm is the perfect place for that," Mercedes added to the conversation.

Zena further explained her desire. "I remember once when I was a little girl that my mother opened our home to a woman in our neighborhood who had been abused. My mother was later abused by my father for taking the woman in. He said it was none of our business. My father kicked the abused woman out onto the streets. I never saw her again. One day I gathered up enough courage to ask my mother about her. She slapped me across my face and told me to never bring that up again." She paused to take a breath.

"Your farm would be the perfect safe haven for people who need it," Ryann said.

"And your husband won't lay a finger on anyone," Paige said. As inappropriate as her comment may have been, everyone ignored her.

"You let me know what you need, and I'll donate the money to help you get started and keep it going, if necessary," Angela commented.

Zena didn't have any words to say. She was bursting with anticipation of what new things the Lord would bring to her life this year. She just looked at Angela and smiled. "Thank you," she mouthed.

Then her eye caught the waitress' eye and waved her over. Before the waitress got there, Zena said, "I almost forgot we were here to eat." To the waitress she said, "How's our food coming? It seems like it's taking a while."

"It's coming out now." She left as quickly as she could. She was almost running.

"She's sure a strange one," Zena said, watching the waitress run away.

Paige

Chatter and prayer requests continued until Paige spoke up rather loudly.

"Finally, here comes the waitress with our food!"

"Here we go," the waitress began placing food around the table. But not everyone got a plate. "I'll be back with the rest." And off she went.

"This isn't what I ordered," Paige said as she looked down at her plate.

"She said she's coming back with the rest of our food. Maybe she just gave you the wrong plate," Mercedes suggested.

"Did any of you order spaghetti with meatballs?" Paige asked.

The ladies who didn't have food yet shook their heads.

They all continued talking as they waited for the rest of their food, but then they began to wonder if their waitress was really coming back.

"Do you think she got lost?" Paige wondered, looking down at the spaghetti in front of her that she did not order and was now growing cold.

"Why don't we pray so the rest of you can eat while your food is still hot?"

Automatically, Kayleigh bowed her head and prayed out loud for their food.

"There she is," Paige stood up so fast that her chair fell over. Fortunately, the noise was enough to make the waitress look in their direction. "Ma'am," Paige called out to her. "My order is incorrect, and we still don't have all our food."

Reluctantly, the waitress walked over to their table. "I'm sorry," she said picking up Paige's plate. "The rest of your food should be coming out right now. Someone in the kitchen accidentally gave it to a take-out order." And just as quickly she ran away again.

"I don't think she wants to talk to us," Paige scowled after her.

Ryann had a strange look on her face. "How could they accidentally give my order to someone else? I know no one ordered the same exact thing as I did."

Because of Ryann's cancer and upcoming treatment, she ordered food that was a little unusual and a lot bland.

Zena

"You guys want to hear a funny story?" Zena asked.

"Is it about one of your kids?" Mercedes asked.

"Two of them actually."

Paige groaned.

"The twins had been a nuisance all day," Zena began. "They were into one thing after another. The baby was screaming to be fed so I had to sit down with her. I sent the boys to the playroom and told them to find something to do."

"That was probably your first mistake," Mackenzie said understanding that two unattended boys could find a lot of trouble to get into in only a few seconds.

"After a few minutes, they were quiet. I know I should have checked on them, but I was reveling in the peace, glad for five uninterrupted minutes. All of a sudden one of the boys came running out of the room, buck naked, dragging a long string of garland that had been on the Christmas tree. It was stuck in his 'cheeks' if you know what I mean."

The ladies began laughing, just imagining the scene.

"He must have been sitting on it for it to get stuck there. A moment later the other one comes out of the room wearing nothing but a Santa hat and the tree skirt from the children's Christmas tree in the playroom."

By now the ladies were all laughing uncontrollably. Zena's animated face, accent, and gestures only added to the story.

"What did the playroom look like when you finally got in there?" Ryann wanted to know.

Zena cringed before she answered, but then she smiled. "It was so worth the five minutes of peace though. I'm choosing to look at it this way: they helped me take down the Christmas decorations that needed to come down anyway."

Paige

"Speaking of a New Year and new beginnings, Angela, I decided I'm going to set you up with my brother. He's about the same age as you."

"Oh, no." Angela held up her hand to stop Paige from talking.

"Come on. It's time for a change."

"I like things the way they are."

"I'll call you with the details."

Before Angela could argue with Paige anymore, Kayleigh dropped a bombshell.

Kayleigh

"My husband is cheating on me." In one way she hoped no one had heard her. In another way, she didn't want to have to repeat her revelation. By the sudden silence of the table, she knew everyone had heard.

"What?"

"Are you okay?"

"You gonna leave him now?"

Except for the last comment, Kayleigh wasn't sure who spoke.

"Now's not the time, Paige," Kayleigh heard Mercedes say.

"Well, it's not a surprise to anyone. How could she not have known?" Paige stated. Everyone but Kayleigh stared Paige down, daring her to speak again.

"It was a surprise to me," Kayleigh said. "Maybe it shouldn't have been, but it was. Maybe I didn't want to see it."

"Oh, honey." Zena, who was sitting next to Kayleigh, put an arm around her shoulders. "Can I do anything for you?"

Kayleigh heard Zena's questions but focused on Paige. "If you knew, why didn't you tell me, Paige?" Kayleigh wondered.

Paige shrugged her shoulders. "I figured you knew." By the look on Paige's face, Kayleigh could tell she regretted the words. Maybe Paige was finally learning.

"I didn't."

"Maybe now is the time to make a change for you," Mercedes lovingly suggested.

"Yeah, you don't have to put up with that," Zena's Greek accent proclaimed.

"You have your proof now."

"A divorce would be acceptable," Ryann said.

Kayleigh knew Ryann was trying to be helpful.

"The day I get divorced is the day I not only give up on my marriage but also the day I give up on God. I believe He has the power to fix this mess I'm in."

Before anyone else could say anything, Kayleigh added, "Excuse me."

She figured she needed a minute, or ten, in the bathroom to compose herself.

Mackenzie

Mackenzie wished she could be as strong as Kayleigh was in the face of adversity. At least what she was going through with her own family wasn't humiliating. She couldn't say the same for Kayleigh.

"What were you thinking, Paige?" Mackenzie asked as soon as Kayleigh was out of earshot.

"I wasn't, I guess." Paige was almost apologetic.

"How did you know he was cheating?" Zena asked.

"I saw him."

"When?" Mercedes' question came next.

"A couple of months ago."

"Why didn't you ever say anything?" Angela sounded a little more sympathetic.

"You guys are always telling me I say the wrong thing." Paige wiped away a tear.

"Well, that hasn't improved," Mackenzie mumbled. She didn't think anyone had heard.

"That's not helping, Mack." Angela now reprimanded her.

It seemed like only a moment before Kayleigh came back and sat down at the table. She looked directly at Paige and said, "There's no need to talk about what you know, Paige. I'm just going to ask that from now on you spend your time praying for him instead of gossiping about him to others."

Mercedes

After about another fifteen tense minutes and still no more food, Mercedes had had enough and decided to take things into her own hands. She forcefully pushed her chair back, making an incredibly awful screeching sound, and stood up.

"I'm going into that kitchen to see what exactly the problem is," she stated.

Paige smiled. "Where's your mercy, Mercy?"

"I show mercy where mercy is due. This is just plain ridiculous." And off she stomped to the kitchen.

"I have got to see this!" Zena exclaimed as she got up and followed at a distance.

"Me, too." Paige also followed along.

Mercedes was shocked at what she saw and what she didn't see. The kitchen was an absolute disaster. There were dirty dishes piled everywhere, giving the impression that someone had gotten some food. A pot of what looked like spaghetti sauce was boiling away on the stove, and probably scorching by the smell that assaulted her.

Then there was the icing on the cake. A man strolled into the kitchen from a door in the back marked "restroom." He was still buttoning his pants. Mercedes gagged.

The waitress bumped Mercedes as she came into the kitchen from who knew where. She certainly hadn't been in the dining room.

At the sight of her, Mercedes raised her voice. "We have been here for two hours. It took forever to get drinks and to even get our orders taken. Now, some of us have food, some of us don't. Not all of the food we did get is right. I will never set foot in this restaurant again, and I will tell everyone I know to not eat here."

When she was done with her tirade, she turned around and stomped back out of the kitchen.

"We're leaving," she said as she stormed past Zena and Paige. Back at the table, she said, "Well, I hate to break up this party, but we need to go." She was speaking of taking Ryann to her first treatment. Both of them stood to leave.

"Can I say a quick prayer first?" Kayleigh asked.

"But we haven't eaten yet," Paige complained.

"Well, at least you had spaghetti and meatballs that you could have eaten." Then some disturbing images flooded her mind. "Never mind. Be glad you didn't eat it."

There was no mistaking the anger in Mercedes' voice. "And we are never coming back here again." Mercedes had used her mom-voice and spoken for them all. "Let's go out to the parking lot to pray."

Everyone pushed back their chairs, walked out to the parking lot, and stood in a circle around Ryann, each one making sure to have a hand on her.

Mercedes took a deep breath to calm herself and get involved in the prayer without all the previous angry thoughts.

"Lord, Ryann is our dear friend. She has some health issues, and we know You are the Great Physician. You have the power to heal her completely at this moment. Lord, give Ryann the strength to get through these treatments. Help us to be the kind of friends she needs us to be. Amen."

A chorus of amens followed Kayleigh's.

"Thanks, everyone," Ryann said as she wiped away the tears in her eyes.

Mercedes stepped back as each of the ladies gave Ryann a hug of encouragement before they left. Although this was not the first time they had all rallied around one of their group, this time it felt different. She let the ladies have their moments. Mercedes would have hers later.

It was only an hour later that the two of them were alone, waiting on the doctor to arrive.

"You doing okay?"

Ryann

Ryann smiled at her sweet friend. She didn't know how she would get through this without Mercedes or the rest of the lunch ladies. She nodded her head in response to Mercedes' question. "I'm doing okay. As well as can be expected, I guess. Nervous."

Mercedes put her arms around Ryann's shoulders. It was a great comfort to Ryann.

Doctor Bernard came in. "I have some good news and some bad news. First of all, this cancer is a bit more aggressive than we first thought. It's good you are starting your treatments today because the sooner we can attack it the better."

Ryann was lost after the words "a little more aggressive than we thought."

"So what does that mean?" Ryann heard Mercedes ask.

She was so thankful Mercedes insisted on coming. She was in no mood to listen and comprehend enough of what the doctor was saying to ask questions or to even know what move to take next. Ryann heard an exchange of words between Mercedes and Doctor Bernard, but what those words were, she didn't know.

The next thing she knew, Mercedes was leading her into a roomful of people, all hooked up to some kind of medical contraptions. And she was next.

All throughout the treatment, pictures of her daughters flashed through her mind. What would happen to them if she died? She shook her head. She had to stop thinking like that. Trying to change the subject in her mind, she looked around the room at the other patients. She was extremely thankful Mercedes had the forethought to warn her that she wouldn't be in a private room. Even knowing this ahead of time she still felt exposed. She wondered if the others felt that way as well or if they were used to it.

Ryann looked down at the floor or up at the ceiling, anywhere but at the other patients. The last thing she wanted was to invade their personal space. She kind of wished she had brought a book or something with her to help pass the time. She made a mental note to do that on her next visit.

Once the treatment was over, Ryann vaguely remembered Mercedes taking her home. She thought there were a few instructions for her daughters, but thankfully it was apparent she didn't have to listen herself. Mercedes took Ryann to her bedroom, helped her change and get into bed. Ryann remembered nothing after that until the next morning, or more accurately, afternoon, Ryann awoke to her oldest daughter sitting in the chair next to the bed.

"Hey, Mom," she smiled.

"Drink," was the only word Ryann was able to get out first.

Jocelyn responded quickly by putting a straw in Ryann's mouth. She closed her eyes as she drank. Water never tasted so good.

"What did Mercedes say?" Ryann was finally able to ask with a raspy voice.

"You might have to have surgery."

So that's what the doctor had said after she had zoned out. Ryann looked to her daughter and could tell she was trying to maintain a brave face.

"It's okay to cry," Ryann assured her, taking her hand.

Suddenly Jocelyn took a deep breath and shook her head. "I don't need to. Let's get you up and get you something to eat."

Ryann really didn't feel like eating, but she knew food was necessary, and she also knew Jocelyn needed to keep busy, so she complied.

Kayleigh

As soon as Kayleigh got wind of what the doctor said about Ryann possibly needing surgery, she organized a prayer meeting for the lunch ladies that evening. She set it up so that everyone would meet at Ryann's that way Ryann would not have to go anywhere.

Ryann was overwhelmed by the prayers and the words of support as her closest friends surrounded her in her time of need. She hadn't felt this supported when her husband had died. Of course, these precious ladies had not all been a part of her life then.

Kayleigh's prayer rendered Ryann completely speechless.

"Dear heavenly Father, You are Jehovah Rapha. You are the ultimate Healer. There is nothing any earthly doctor can do that can compare to Your healing hand. I pray You touch my dear servant friend, Ryann. Take this cancer from her body. Heal her so that she does not have to have surgery. Make a miracle of her so she can share that testimony to all with whom she comes in contact."

Chapter 6

Above all, love each other deeply, because love covers over a multitude of sins. Offer hospitality to one another without grumbling. Each of you should use whatever gift you have received to serve others, as faithful stewards of God's grace in its various forms. - 1 Peter 4:8-10

February

Mackenzie

Mackenzie really didn't feel like going to lunch. She just wanted to stay home with her boys and hold them tight. The diagnosis the doctor had given for her baby boy had not been good. If she could just cuddle up with him under a blanket for the rest of his life, that suited her just fine. Of course, his life wouldn't last anywhere near long enough.

Kayleigh

Kayleigh didn't even know why she bothered with the sunglasses. She wasn't sure the ladies believed her story about the eye doctor's last time. She supposed she didn't have to pretend around her friends. It was the stares of strangers she couldn't stand. It was like they would see deep into her mind and know all her secrets.

"Get your eyes dilated again?" Paige asked with attitude as soon as she saw her.

"Sure did," Kayleigh said with a little bit of attitude herself, but they both knew it wasn't true.

Subtlety was not Paige's strongest trait. "Is there a reason you had to have another test so soon?"

Kayleigh knew Paige was looking for information.

"No," was her response.

Paige just stared at her. Even though Kayleigh was grateful Paige had stopped being her usual vocal self, she didn't exactly care for the look she was receiving either.

"He needs your prayers right now more than he needs your judgment," Kayleigh whispered harshly. She needed to at least feel as if she had the upper hand.

"You have every right to leave him, you know."

"That may be your conviction, not mine."

Kayleigh now turned to her opposite side partly to end the conversation with Paige and partly because Zena laid a hand on her arm.

"I've been where you are right now. I know what you're going through," Zena said.

She felt that people judged her when they found out he was cheating on her. It was almost as if Kayleigh could read their minds.

I wonder what she did to make him be unfaithful.

Has she cheated on him?

What is she doing, or not doing, that is making him so unhappy?

What did she do to make him so mad he found it necessary to hit her?

Kayleigh was tired of it all. Many days she wished she could just disappear and no one would even notice that she had gone. Kayleigh decided to keep her mouth shut. She was angry and felt like people were judging her along with her husband and his actions, wondering what she had done wrong to deserve the treatment she was receiving from him. But, she had done nothing wrong. She didn't deserve it. She wished her friends would just do as she asked: pray for his salvation, and pray that she would be a good testimony to him in the meantime.

She always tried to be an encourager to others, but sometimes she needed to be encouraged herself. Most days Kayleigh may have appeared strong on the outside, while on the inside she was falling apart, wishing she didn't have to go through it alone. She found herself sending up a quick prayer for understanding. *Lord, please help them understand, or at least accept, my position on the matter.*

God answered that prayer immediately.

Zena

Zena felt the need to stand up and get everyone else's attention.

"Before food comes I'd like to take a few moments to pray for Kayleigh. I don't think we've been very supportive of her decisions, and God has been convicting me of that."

The ladies all looked at Kayleigh, who was still wearing her sunglasses.

Zena, still standing, took Kayleigh's hand in her own, as well as Mackenzie's who was sitting on her other side. She waited until each of them was holding the hands of ladies on either side.

"Lord, our friend Kayleigh has a request she wants to lay before Your feet. It's no surprise to you that Jeff isn't the best husband in the world. He needs You, Lord. I pray that he would be persuaded to come to church and get to know You on a personal level as Kayleigh does. Pray that Kayleigh's sweet spirit would be the influence he needs or put someone else in his path who can reach him. May this coming Sunday be the one. Amen."

"And help him to realize his wife is not a punching bag."

Zena opened her eyes and looked straight at Paige with the look she usually reserved for her unruly children. It must have worked on Paige as well since Zena could see Paige's lips tighten together as if she was trying not to let any more surly words come out of her mouth.

Because of Paige, it took Zena a moment to realize that Kayleigh still held tightly to her hand. Kayleigh squeezed Zena's hand and mouthed 'thank you.' Zena just squeezed her hand back in response before she sat down to enjoy her lunch.

Paige

Paige felt the need to change the subject and to put the focus on someone else. Besides she had a secret she needed to divulge quickly.

"So, tonight's the night right, Angela?" Her voice was sing-songy, on the verge of the screechy, but she didn't care. She was excited, even if she was the only one.

Angela stared at Paige and then rolled her eyes.

"Can't you be even a little bit excited?" Paige wondered.

"No," Angela answered simply.

"Oh, pooh! Tom doesn't seem to be the least bit excited about this either. I just wanted to do something nice for you guys."

Angela smiled at her. "I'm going, aren't I?"

"Yeah, but you don't have to act like you're doing me a favor." Paige really wanted a relationship to develop between Tom and Angela. Angela was one of her dearest friends; one of those women who accepted Paige for who she was, quirks and all.

"I'm going, and I don't even have a bad attitude," Angela stated.

"Yes, but you seem a bit leery."

"Wouldn't you be a bit leery to go out and meet a strange man for dinner? I think a little leeriness is healthy," Angela said.

"But he's my brother..."

"That you just recently met," Angela interrupted.

"He could be a psycho," Ryann added her thoughts to the conversation.

"Thanks," Angela gave Ryann a look of mock appreciation.

Ryann winked.

"He's a missionary," Paige found it necessary to remind them.

"So he says," Zena piped in.

"Would you guys stop? It's going to be great. You wait and see. Besides the evening is all paid for, so you have to go." Her last statement was directed at Angela alone. "In fact, I was so excited about all of you meeting him that I invited him to lunch today."

"What?" Everyone had the same reaction at the same time.

Paige ignored them as her attention was drawn to the restaurant entrance. "Oh, look, here he comes now." A man that could only be described as tall, dark, and handsome, even if he was her brother, walked in.

"That's your brother?" Angela gasped.

"Yep." Paige could not have been more proud of him and not only for his good looks either. In the last couple of months she had discovered he had a great heart too.

One that would mesh perfectly with Angela's.

Angela

Angela could not believe her eyes. In fact, she couldn't help but just stare at him. She only half heard as Paige introduced him to each one of the ladies. Angela was standing behind the towering Mackenzie, so she knew he didn't see her at first. In fact, she was the last one Paige introduced him to.

"And, last but not least," Paige took hold of Angela's arm and pulled her fully out from behind Mackenzie. "There's no need to hide. This is…"

"Hi, Tom," Angela said before Paige could finish the introductions herself.

"Angela!" He said it not as a question but in surprise. He immediately looked to Paige. "This is your friend Angela that you've been trying to set me up with?"

Angela could tell by the look on Paige's face, and by the fact that she seemed speechless, that she was surprised and confused.

"What? Wait, you already know each other?"

Angela and Tom looked at each other. "For about ten years or so?" Angela looked at Tom for confirmation.

He nodded. "That sounds about right."

"Well, there has to be a story here. Let's sit down and eat so we can hear it," Zena encouraged.

As they rearranged spots so Tom could sit between Angela and Paige, Angela noted that Paige looked upset.

"Don't be so disappointed, Paige. Suddenly my wariness of going on a blind date has dissipated completely."

"I'm glad I wasn't the only one who was leery," Tom said.

"And this is only your first set up by Paige," Angela joked and winked at the younger woman. "She's made a habit of blind dates for my life."

"I'm sure she would have done the same for you, Tom, if you had only been around," Kayleigh stated.

"So, what's the story?" Ryann grinned at her friend. "How did you two meet?"

"The mission board," Angela simply said.

"There has to be more to the story than that," Mercedes pushed her plate out of the way and leaned forward as if eager to hear all the details.

Angela bobbed her head back and forth. "The missions group I work for assigned me to be on his board. I've also been personally helping to support him and the work he does. In fact, I financially adopted one of the little girls in the orphanage he works with."

"Lily." Tom looked at Angela and smiled.

The way he smiled at her made her stomach feel as if there was a roller coaster twisting and turning at full speed down there. Maybe this date night wouldn't be so bad. Perhaps she should keep an open mind, especially now that she knew who her date actually was and not a psycho.

Mercedes, ever the mother of the group, started asking Tom questions. "So, Tom, how long have you been a missionary?"

"It wasn't too long after my mom left with Paige that another woman came into my dad's life, but this woman was so different. She was always smiling. Her eyes shone with a light that was completely foreign to both Dad and me. Her face literally glowed, and it wasn't makeup. I had never seen anything like it before, but I was definitely attracted to her." Tom must have realized what he said and corrected himself. "Not attracted in a weird sort of way."

Angela giggled at the looks on the other ladies' faces. She had heard his story before and quietly listened as he continued.

"She made us want to be around her. She brought a happiness into our lives we had never known before. And then one day she told us what was so different about her. It was Jesus Christ."

Angela looked at Paige who had her face resting in her hands, listening with rapt attention.

"Tamara, that's her name, invited us to church, and Dad and I haven't been the same since. We both accepted Christ. We were both baptized. We both got involved in the church and its activities. We grew in the Lord together. It's been an amazing journey."

"What happened to Tamara?" Paige wondered.

Tom smiled. "They eventually got married. She made my dad happier than I'd ever seen him. He was truly a changed man, and that's what he always shared when he was asked to give his testimony." Tom then tilted his head to one side. "In fact, he shared his story with everyone who would listen. When my dad said he was going shopping it wasn't for actual food or clothes or other necessities, it was to see who he could find to talk to. The man didn't know a stranger. He was like that until the day he died."

Paige stared at Tom with a grin on her face. Angela wondered what it was like for her to learn about her father, a man she had really never known. She was sure there would be much sharing of pictures and stories in the coming days.

When the ladies finished with their interrogation of poor Tom, Mercedes finally turned to Angela and said, "I find him acceptable for you to date."

While the other ladies around the table laughed, Angela responded with, "Thanks, Mom," which made everyone laugh even harder.

Paige merely sat there looking perfectly pleased with herself.

Ryann

Lunch ended on a high note. Angela was looking forward to her now not-so-blind date with Tom. Mercedes approved of the relationship. Ryann didn't doubt that Paige was already planning a wedding. With so much happiness around her, Ryann was feeling a little jealous. Everyone else's lives seemed so sure. Hers was anything but that.

Mackenzie

After lunch, Mackenzie picked up Cameron, Mrs. Schuyler said, "He seemed a little draggy today"
"He didn't sleep too well last night."

Mackenzie had not explained Cameron's health issues to Mrs. Schuyler. She wondered if perhaps she should since the sweet neighbor lady took time out of her day to care for him, neither expecting nor wanting anything in return. Mackenzie had tried paying her, but Mrs. Schuyler would not take it.

"It's more than enough to be able to enjoy his laughter and smiling face," she had said. "It's been so long since any of my children were that little. I enjoy every moment of it."

Mackenzie could only pray that the Lord would bless Mrs. Schuyler in a way that only He could.

"I think we might both go home and take a nap." Mackenzie picked Cameron up and snuggled him close, trying not to have to explain about his situation. At least not yet. She would have to do it soon. Mrs. Schuyler would be just as devastated as Mackenzie at the impending loss. The older woman should at least have a heads up. It was only fair.

"See you later," Mackenzie waved as she turned to walk home with Cameron.

As she got closer to her front door she noticed a rather large box sitting there. She scrunched her eyes together wondering what it could be. There certainly was no money available for ordering anything. Her name was written across the tape that held the box shut. Because of that, there was no mistaking it was meant for her.

Cameron had fallen asleep in her arms on the short walk home, so she laid him on the couch and covered him with his "Zena quilt" as he called it. Smiling down at him as she pushed the hair out of his eyes, she once again threw up a quick prayer to God, the same exact one-sentence prayer she had uttered countless times recently.

"He needs a miracle, Lord."

Finally, curiosity got the better of her, and she went to drag the box off the porch and into the house. Its contents made her gasp. It was full of food. As she pulled out one item after another, she noticed many of them were favorites of the boys. There was enough food to last them at least a month if she was careful at rationing it out. And if she gave preteen, always hungry, bottomless pit Jordan a speech about recreational eating. Mackenzie collapsed in a chair at the kitchen table, overcome with gratitude. There was only one thing she could do, and that was pray.

"Lord, I don't know where this all came from, but I give You all the praise and thanks. You have definitely sent angels to watch over us."

After these words, all she could mutter was "thank you" over and over again, along with shedding plenty of tears. She couldn't help but wonder who had sent it. Angela would sometimes bring her groceries, more often than not she simply handed her a gift card. It couldn't have been Zena; she didn't buy any already prepared foods. There was also the fact that she had been with all of the lunch ladies for the past couple of hours. It couldn't have been any of them.

"Mom, I'm home!" Jordan shouted, allowing the door to slam.

Normally she would have fussed at him about that, but the noise didn't seem to have disturbed sleeping Cameron at all, so she let it go. She tried to dry her eyes quickly by wiping them on the sleeve of her shirt, but an ever-observant Jordan didn't miss it.

"Mom, what's..." His words stopped short when he saw the pile of food on the table. "Where did all that come from?"

Mackenzie could only shrug her shoulders and shake her head.

He started picking through stuff. "I like these. And look, name brand cookies. These are good."

Mackenzie placed a hand on his as he reached for another item. When he looked directly into her face, she asked, "You didn't tell anyone did you?"

"No, I didn't."

A month ago she realized she needed to fill Jordan in on what was going on in their household. He had begun complaining about all they didn't have. She didn't want him telling his friends at school there was hardly any food in the house. She also didn't want him getting picked on because his mom didn't have a job. Kids could be ruthless sometimes. Surprisingly, Jordan had taken the news like the man he was becoming. He had even offered to get a job.

After he answered her, he looked down.

"Jordan, what is it?"

He looked up at her with tears in his eyes. "Ever since you told me you lost your job, I've been praying a lot more. I prayed for Cameron. I prayed that God would provide what we needed." His voice faded away as if he couldn't say anymore.

Mackenzie knew it was hard for twelve-year-old boys to show such emotions, so she stood back and said nothing.

After another moment Jordan sniffed and held out his arms to encompass all the groceries on the table before them. "Look at this!" His voice squeaked in a pubescent manner.

Mackenzie could bear it no longer. She reached over and put her arms around him. He reciprocated and they cried together. Mackenzie cried that God had heard and answered Jordan's prayers. She cried that Jordan saw that it was God answering his prayers. She cried because of the godly man he was becoming. They were all happy tears.

Then something dawned on her. No wonder all the boys' favorites had been included in the box. No one knew them better than their heavenly Father.

Mercedes

After yet another heated conversation with Annie, if one could actually call it a conversation, Mercedes was more discouraged than ever. She never meant for their talk to go the way it did, but she had to be honest and realize the sour turn had not been her fault.

In an attempt to at least maintain their relationship, Mercedes had called to see how Sadie, her granddaughter was feeling with her pregnancy.

"Are you calling so you can gloat?" Annie had spit the words out with a fierceness and hatred Mercedes didn't know her daughter possessed.

Mercedes stuttered, surprised by the accusation. "Wha… Wha… No. I just wanted to check on her."

"Yeah, right! I know how you are, thinking that you're all high and mighty and perfect."

Mercedes found her spunk. "You know that's not true. I've spent your entire life proving that to you."

"I know you talk about your hateful daughter with your Christian friends. Don't think what you say doesn't make its way back to me."

Mercedes was flabbergasted. She didn't know what to say. The only ones she ever spoke to about Annie were the lunch ladies, and even then it was only to ask them to pray. Where would Annie have heard things Mercedes said?

Mercedes never got the chance to ask Annie exactly what she had heard since Annie hung up on her. Mercedes tossed the phone down on the couch beside her. When would she ever be able to break through the wall Annie had built between them?

Chapter 7

And let us consider how we may spur one another on toward love and good deeds. - Hebrews 10:24

March

Kayleigh

Kayleigh lay still in bed. She was waiting to hear Jeff leave the house for work. Last night she had made his lunch and put it in the fridge so she wouldn't have to get up in the morning. Jeff had been so testy lately that she was making a point of staying away from him whenever she could without causing him to be even angrier. That was a delicate balance. It didn't take much these days to tip the scales to the negative. Last night had not been a great night, so Kayleigh was being extra careful. It was lunch day, and she didn't want to have to hide behind her sunglasses for the third month in a row.

Even when she heard the front door slam shut she didn't jump out of bed right away. Many times Jeff came back in the house to grab something he forgot. When she heard his truck peel out of the driveway, she figured it was safe to get up. She threw back the covers and sat up. Pretending to be asleep was a good choice if Jeff's stomping around was any indication of his attitude. She sighed. Oh, how Kayleigh wished things were different.

Kayleigh walked out to the living room to where she had left her Bible and her little black book. She needed to spend some considerable time in prayer today. Jeff needed prayer. Satan and his cohorts never took a day off, so she couldn't afford to take a day off either.

"Lord, there are so many issues I want to bring before You today, first I want to give You praise. Thank You for being my God. Thank You for protecting me last night. There are so many things for which be thankful. Lord, You know my heart and that I try to thank You each day when each moment arises.

"I thank You for giving me Jeff as a husband, but he needs You, God. Only You know what is truly going on in his heart and mind. Help him to feel Your presence in his life."

Kayleigh spent quite some time in prayer mentioning each of her friends by name and the specific issues she knew about. She also prayed for any unspoken requests she may not have had a clue about.

"Lord, there are things we all keep to ourselves. There are struggles to come that we have no inkling about yet. Wrap Your arms of protection around each one of my precious friends today. Bless our fellowship this afternoon. Amen."

When she was done praying she stood up and said, "Now I can start my day."

Ryann

Ryann had to giggle inwardly at Mercedes. Every time Mercedes brought her to the hospital for treatment she had to spend some time in the gym.

"You're just using me for my cancer," Ryann teased.

"Your attempt at humor and the situation is unsuccessful," Mercedes said with no hint of a smile on her face. "They just have wonderful equipment here that I don't always get to use. I'm making the most of every opportunity."

"You exercise to an extreme," Ryann commented back.

"I'm just trying to keep healthy, okay?" It was really more of a statement than a question.

"Mm-hm." Ryann still wasn't buying it.

Then Mercedes stopped everything she was doing and looked Ryann right in the face. "You really want to know the truth of it?"

"I'd love to hear it." Ryann was trying to stay upbeat.

"It calms my nerves."

"Calms your nerves? You're probably one of the calmest, levelheaded women I know."

"On the outside."

Ryann didn't know how to respond to that.

"You're one of my best friends in the world. Do you know what it feels like to sit here and watch you suffer through these abominable treatments?"

"You don't have to come," Ryann said tenderly, seeing a different side to Mercedes.

Mercedes sort of smiled. "Being here brings back memories for me and not good ones. I know exactly what you're going through, and..."

"I'm sorry," Ryann said. "I never gave it a thought. You don't have to bring me any more. I'll have Jocelyn drive me from now on."

"Oh, no," Mercedes began. "I *want* to be here with you, for you, but it's a little painful at the same time."

Ryann studied her friend for a moment. She thought she understood what Mercedes was trying to say. She grabbed one of her hands and gave it a squeeze. "I'm glad you're here."

Mercedes smiled a genuine, warm smile.

"There's the Mercy I know. Now, go get your exercise in. I'll still be here, attached to this thing, when you get back. But promise me you'll eat something fattening. You're wasting away to nothing."

Mercedes gave Ryann's hand pat before she left. Ryann watched her leave. There went a true friend.

True friends was not an area of her life where she was lacking. When her phone chirped, she picked it up to see a text from Kayleigh.

Just wanted to let you know I'm praying for you today.

Ryann couldn't help but smile in spite of her circumstances. She texted back. *Thanks, friend. You know I need all the prayers I can get.*

No. True friends were definitely not in short supply. On the other hand, she often felt as if her prayer life was lacking. She was grateful for friends like Kayleigh who could remind her to pray without actually telling her she wasn't praying enough. And there was no time like the present to fix that. She wasn't going anywhere for a while.

"Lord, I thank You for the wonderful women You've put in my life. Each of them means so much to me." She put her head back to rest and closed her eyes to continue praying for everyone and everything that came to her mind. She spent her time praying for each of them by name. Her time spent in prayer passed so quickly, Ryann was surprised at Mercedes' return.

"How are you doing, kiddo?"

"I'm ready to go home."

"I understand that."

They spent the rest of Ryann's time in companionable silence, Mercedes holding Ryann's hand and giving it a squeeze every once in a while.

Yes, this was true friendship.

Mercedes

At lunch the week after Ryann's treatments, Mercedes decided to ask her friends to pray for a request that had been on her heart for some time.

"I need prayer right now, and I don't know who to ask. Maybe it's just that I don't want to tell anyone else," Mercedes began.

"What is it?" Kayleigh asked, already getting out her little, black book.

Mercedes looked at each of her friends and noted that they were eagerly waiting to hear what she had to say. That made her smile in spite of the turmoil she was feeling.

"It's Annie, my daughter." She paused for a moment. "Now that I'm thinking of the words to say it doesn't seem all that important."

"If it's important to you, it's important to God and to us," Ryann said.

Everyone agreed.

"Just because our children are grown and out of our homes, doesn't mean they should ever be out of our hearts or our prayers," Zena added.

Mercedes smiled at her. Then she shared with everyone what was on her heart. "Well, Annie is dating someone. There's no immorality between them that I know of, believe it or not. I'm just not sure this guy makes her a better person. They don't seem to complement each other at all. He certainly is not a bad person, but I'm afraid that if they get married he won't be the spiritual head of the household. I know Annie didn't have a male example because I never married her father, but I think she missed out on something special. I think it's necessary. But then again, maybe I'm completely wrong. Maybe he's the one I've been praying for all these years. Maybe I just don't know him well enough to make an informed opinion. He seems to like her kids and doesn't seem to mind the thought of being a grandfather at the ripe old age of thirty-five."

Mercedes suddenly stopped, realizing she was rambling. Before anyone was able to comment, she added, "See, it's silly."

"It's not silly," Paige said.

"We will all definitely be praying for you," Angela said from across the table.

"I understand how you feel. My children may be young, but I have prayed for them, since the day they were born, that they would one day find a godly mate. It's such a huge and important decision."

Zena's words made Mercedes feel better. At least she wasn't the only one who worried over who her children married.

Angela

For Angela, lunch day was "the day after." She and Tom had gone out on their first official date after their initial "blind" date that Paige set up. Paige had blabbed all about it to everyone even after Angela had told her not to.

She arrived late for lunch hoping that would help deter comments, but she was wrong. She was barely in the door when all eyes were on her and the questions began. She wasn't even sure how it happened because it happened so quickly, but suddenly Paige was directly in front of her, holding her hands, and begging like a dog.

"Details! Details! How did it go?"

Angela pulled her hands away from Paige and walked around her. As she got settled in her seat she said, "I don't kiss and tell."

"Oh, come on! You have to."

Angela looked up to see Zena with her own set of puppy dog eyes.

She thought she'd humor them, or maybe more so herself, by saying, "Everything went fine."

"We need more than that," Mackenzie said uncharacteristically loud.

Angela conceded, knowing this was a losing battle. "It was nice, and we will more than likely see each other again."

"Of course you will. You work together." Paige's demeanor told Angela she was not satisfied with that pitiful answer.

Apparently, neither was Zena. "Outside of work?"

Angela gave one simple nod of her head. "Yes, outside of work."

Paige clapped her hands together. "I knew you two were perfect for each other!"

"We haven't exactly planned the wedding yet," Angela stated.

"'Yet' being the operative word in that sentence." Ryann looked at her and smiled.

"Don't worry." Paige piped up. "I've already started on that."

Zena

While the others were busy listening to Paige prattle on about all the things she had planned for Angela's wedding that wasn't even an actuality yet, Zena made a private moment with Ryann.

"I know you're probably not in the mood for much celebrating, but I made something for your birthday."

Ryann half smiled. "You're right, I'm not."

"But every birthday is worth celebrating, from the first to the last and all the ones in between." Zena handed Ryann a small gift bag. "I thought you might need this soon."

Ryann pulled out a hat Zena had crocheted with her in mind. It was pink, Ryann's favorite color, with a darker pink crocheted flower on the side.

"I hope it fits," Zena said.

Ryann didn't say anything, she couldn't for the tears, but she was able to reach over and gave Zena a hug.

"This is so beautiful and thoughtful. Thank you!" she whispered.

"You're welcome."

Wiping her eyes and taking a breath, Ryann said. "Now I need to lighten the mood." She pulled the hat down on her head. "How do I look?"

Zena smiled. "As wonderful as ever."

Paige

One evening, Paige was monotonously stuffing envelopes for her job when she heard the doorbell ring. In the quiet house, it seemed extra shrilly and grated on her nerves. Her grammy had dozed off in her reading chair and just about jumped out of it at the sound.

"Who could that be at this hour?"

Paige smiled as she got up to answer the door. "This hour" was exactly 6:30. She couldn't help but wonder if she would be like her grammy when she became an old woman.

"Tom!" Paige welcomed him with open arms.

"Don't get up, Grammy," Tom said as he walked over to give her a hug.

Paige had enjoyed watching Tom and their grandma get to know each other. Paige felt her family was growing finally, one person at a time.

"What are you doing here at this hour?" Grammy asked.

Paige couldn't help but snicker when Tom glanced at his watch and then looked to her.

"Am I interrupting dinner?"

"You aren't interrupting anything. What brings you here?"

Tom made himself comfortable on the couch, and Paige plopped down next to him sitting Indian style.

He shrugged his shoulders. "I was just in the area and thought I'd stop in to see you girls. Also, I wanted to see what wedding plans you had cooking."

That statement was meant to tease Paige. He winked at her.

"What wedding plans?" Grammy asked.

Tom smirked and tilted his head in Paige's direction.

"I was just joking…sort of. Apparently, Paige has mine and Angela's wedding all planned out, even though we've only been out on a couple of dates and are not engaged just yet." Tom put enough emphasis on the words "are not" there was no way Paige could miss his meaning.

"I just got a little excited. Sorry." She crossed her arms as an obstinate child might.

"Girly," Grammy reverted to her longtime nickname for Paige. "Your mouth is going to get you in trouble someday. I keep telling you that."

Tom looked extremely shocked. "You mean she hasn't gotten in trouble for it yet?"

Paige pressed her lips together and narrowed her eyes at him. "Is this what it's like to have a brother? Your sarcasm isn't appreciated."

Tom winked again. "You know you love having me around."

Yeah. Dang it! Paige did love having him around. The only problem was she now knew what she had been missing all these years and felt cheated.

The three conversed for a while until Grammy started yawning constantly.

"I'll leave you girls alone to do…whatever it is you girls do." Tom got up to leave. He then turned to Paige and with the toss of his head toward the front door asked, "Walk me out?"

Paige thought it was strange, but pretty much everything in this new brother/sister relationship was strange.

As they walked down the porch steps toward his car, Tom said, "Can I ask you to not go overboard with the wedding planning just yet?"

When Paige started to interrupt him, he held up his hand for her to stop talking.

"I know you're excited about my relationship with Angela. I am too, but we need some time to go slow and figure everything out. Neither one of us knows yet what God's will is in this situation, and it's His opinion that matters most. I don't want to hurt Angela; we have to tread very lightly given our professional relationship. I don't want to lose her from my board, and I don't want things to become awkward between us in case a deeper relationship doesn't work out." He paused before adding, "Got it?"

"I don't particularly care for it, but yeah, I got it."

Tom smiled then and gave her a light punch across the nose as an adult would do to a child. She wasn't a child and didn't appreciate being treated like one, with the gesture or the speech. But she would keep her word, and she wouldn't say a word about wedding plans out loud to anyone. However, that would certainly not keep her from continuing her planning. Her Pinterest board would still be seeing some wedding planning action.

"See ya," Tom said as he slid into his car.

Paige lifted her hand in a wave as he drove away. As soon as he was out of sight, she went inside to help her grandma get ready for bed and finish stuffing her envelopes. Then she could do some more wedding planning.

Mackenzie

Mackenzie paced back and forth in her tiny living room. She switched Cameron from one shoulder to another as she tried to soothe the crying little boy. It had been a couple of hours since she had given him some medicine. It should have started working by now. The fever should have at least abated somewhat, but it hadn't.

Glancing at the clock she groaned. 3 AM. She hated to call Mrs. Schuyler, but the only other option was to wake up Jordan and take him along to the emergency room. She had hoped to wait until morning so she could take Cameron to the clinic, but that didn't seem to be an option either. The one good thing about going to the emergency room was that she wouldn't have to pay for it right away; they would send a bill later. She could worry about finances then. Right now her little boy needed some help.

She pulled out her phone and dialed Mrs. Schuyler's number.

"I'll be right over, honey," was how she answered the phone.

How grateful Mackenzie was for the sweet lady. A gift was certainly in order, but Mackenzie decided she would think about that later.

Chapter 8

There is nothing better than a friend, unless it's a friend with chocolate. - Anonymous

April

Paige

"They're going to be so mad at me for being late again!" Paige talked to herself as she waited at the stoplight just before the restaurant. She willed the light to turn green so she could get where she was going. She always looked forward to lunch days, but especially today as it was her birthday month. Mack was sure to have made something special for her.

As soon as the light turned green, she stepped on the gas a little harder than necessary. She cringed as her tires squealed a little. They squealed again as she hit the brakes hard and took the turn into the restaurant parking lot.

Huffing and puffing a little, she flopped down in the empty chair next to Mackenzie. "Sorry I'm late. I'm not a multitasker."

"What?" Mackenzie shook her head as if she didn't understand.

"I was trying to put lotion on while I was driving and dumped it down the front of my shirt. I had to stop and buy a new one."

Mackenzie gave her head a slight shake in disbelief. "Well, since you're finally here, I have something for you."

"You never disappoint." Paige received a small package at the same time she leaned in for a hug.

"What is it?" Kayleigh asked.

"Don't keep us in suspense!" Ryann clapped her hands in excitement.

Paige tore away the paper and gasped. "Oh, Mack, how did you do this?"

"Your grammy and I were in cahoots. I went over one day when I knew you wouldn't be there, and she let me borrow the old picture you had of your brother. I scanned it and did some touching up before enlarging and printing it."

For probably the first time in her life, Paige found herself speechless. She reached over to give Mackenzie another hug; only this one was longer and tighter. When she finally pulled away she didn't even bother wiping away the tears that were running down her face.

"This is the best gift ever!" She held the frame to her chest.

"Let me see!"

Everyone else around the table wanted to sneak a peek at Mackenzie's latest handiwork.

"I'm glad you like it," Mackenzie smiled.

"I will look at it every single day and not only think of Tom but you also." She zoned out of the conversation around the table as she took a few more moments to enjoy her gift.

Zena

"Have you thought any more about your shelter?" Ryann asked.

Zena wondered if she looked as ridiculous as her face felt, but she couldn't help the huge smile. It was exciting. "Yes! Cooper and I have been doing a lot of talking and taking a lot of notes. I actually had to start a binder to hold everything and keep it all together. In some ways, there's a lot of red tape, which can be discouraging, but we're trying to muddle through. We wanted to keep the shelter as much of a secret as possible for the sake of the ladies who would be coming there. We still have a lot to decide. I covet everyone's prayers."

"I'll definitely be praying," Ryann assured her.

"Have you thought about having it be a ministry of the church?" Angela asked. "I'm not certain what all would be involved in that either, but if you work under the umbrella of the church maybe there would be at least a little less red tape."

Zena pressed her lips together and nodded her head. "That might be an idea. I'll have to look into it."

"Whatever you do make sure to consult with a lawyer," Mercedes added from her end of the table. "A good lawyer will be able to help you with any of the red tape but also make sure you, your family, and your property are all protected."

Zena nodded again. "Good idea. I'll call Pastor tonight, run our ideas by him, and ask if he knows of a lawyer who could help."

A shelter for battered women was so important to Zena. What thrilled her even more was that Cooper was fully into it as well. He had been throwing out more ideas than Zena had been. He wanted to build a couple of cabins where the women could stay. He was already working on enlarging their vegetable garden area. He wanted to build a summer kitchen close to the garden where the women could learn how to preserve food while keeping all the heat out of the main kitchen. Cooper often complained about the heat canning brought to the kitchen, but Zena never heard a griping word while he was enjoying the fruits of their labor. He was also helping Zena map out flower gardens where women could work, but also find peace and relaxation. Working together, as long as their plans were also God's plans, Zena knew they could accomplish anything.

Angela

"So, Angela," Paige began, "You've been awful hard to get a hold of lately. What have you been up to?"

Angela sometimes wished a hole would open up and swallow Paige, but then there were the times she just wanted to hug her, especially for "introducing" her to Tom.

"I've been a little busy."

"Yeah, I've noticed you don't answer your phone anymore," Ryann sent a wink in her direction.

"I didn't realize I was at your beck and call." She said it with a little twinkle in her eye.

"Have you been spending too much time with a certain young man?" Zena teased.

"Apparently you all think I am," Angela said with a laugh.

"We are just teasing," Kayleigh said. "I've been praying for you, that the Lord would bless your relationship and make you two completely happy together if that's where you're going to be."

Angela smiled. "Well, your prayers are working, Kayleigh. We are extremely happy together. We're going slow and taking the time to get to know each other in a different way. We've always known each other in a working relationship, never having an inkling for anything else. We're doing a lot of talking on a more personal level and trying to see if there is anything romantic in there."

"Is there?" Mercedes asked.

Angela couldn't help but smile. She tilted her head back and forth a couple of times. "Maybe." She felt her face flush as if she were a teenage girl who had a crush on a boy. *Well,* she thought, *teenager, no. Crush, yes.* There was a part of her who believed it would develop into more than that.

Paige clasped her hands in front of her chest and wiggled her body back and forth.

She's as giddy as a schoolgirl, Angela thought to herself. *But then I suppose I am as well.*

Angela thought it was about time she said it. "Thank you, Paige!"

126

Paige smiled back. "You're welcome." Then, after a pause, she added, "Sis."

"I think I'm hearing wedding bells in the distance," Zena put a hand up to her ear and turned her head to pretend to listen.

"Enough about me. I'm thinking someone else has some news to share."

"Who?" Everyone wanted to know. Everyone, except Kayleigh.

Kayleigh

"Kayleigh," Angela answered. "Just look at her face."

Kayleigh suddenly felt self-conscious as everyone stared at her. She had felt like a smiling fool. She had to have known someone would pick up on it. Still, she was trying to be cautious with her heart and her hopes.

"So, what's your smile about?" Angela encouraged her. "I didn't see you in church on Sunday."

"Oh? We were there." Kayleigh was purposely evasive, but Zena caught her little two-letter word.

"We?"

Kayleigh smiled even bigger if that were possible. "Yes, we."

"I didn't see you," Paige said in an almost accusatory voice.

Kayleigh didn't even care about Paige's attitude. Nothing could dampen her spirits. "We sat in the very back. The only way Jeff said he would go would be if we came in late and left early. He didn't want to talk to anyone."

"How did you get him to come? What did you say to convince him?" Ryann wondered.

Kayleigh shrugged her shoulders. "I never said a word, at least not to him. My knees have felt a little bruised lately, though." She referred to the many hours she spent in prayer. Jeff had been constantly on her mind and in her heart. The pull to pray for him was powerful. There were days she would be puttering around the house and she would have to stop and pray right then and there. She figured God must have been working on Jeff's conscience.

"I hope it's also because of the prayers you all promised to send God on his behalf," Kayleigh added.

"Do you think he'll come back next week?" Angela wondered.

Kayleigh shrugged her shoulders. "I hope so. He didn't say he definitely wouldn't, and he didn't seem angry afterward, which I was afraid he would be. In fact, he took me out to lunch after services. That's the first time we've had a date in I don't know when."

"Awww! Was it nice?" Zena asked, smiling.

Kayleigh thought for a moment before speaking. She looked her friends in the eyes as she spoke. "I think it was the nicest afternoon we've ever had." She wiped away a tear, a happy tear.

Mercedes put her hand on Kayleigh's arm. "I'm so happy for you."

"Thanks," Kayleigh smiled back. "It's because of all of your prayers. I thank you for that. 'The effective prayers of a righteous man (or woman) availeth much.'"

Ryann shook her head. "It wasn't us. It's because of your persistently sweet testimony. I apologize for all of our attitudes towards Jeff. Where we believed you should have dumped him long ago, you believed you could win him over."

Kayleigh shook her head. "One visit to church hasn't exactly won him over yet. I need all of you to continue praying."

"We will, and we will be even more earnest about it this time." Paige looked at the others sitting around the table and then back to Kayleigh. "At least I will," she added quietly.

Ryann

Ryann was so happy for Kayleigh. This was something Ryann knew Kayleigh had prayed long and hard about. Ryann felt a twinge of conviction knowing she had not prayed about Kayleigh and Jeff as often or nearly as earnestly as she should have.

And think about all the times she sends me a text or Scripture verse to let me know she's praying for me!

In many of those moments Ryann hadn't shared anything with anyone, yet Kayleigh was in tune to God's leading at exactly the right time.

Lord, nudge my heart to pray more, she quickly sent up a request as Paige spoke to her.

"Is that all you're going to eat?"

Ryann looked down at the plate in front of her. She had only ordered a small salad, and she wasn't even sure she could eat all of that.

"Yeah. The treatments leave me feeling kind of blah. When I do eat something, I'm trying to make sure it's something that will actually nourish my body and not just be a pleasure food."

"You should eat what sounds good," Mercedes said from across the table.

Ryann smirked. "I really want to eat some piping hot, salty French fries, but after frying, potatoes can hardly be called a nutritious vegetable."

"You're going to lose some weight more than likely," Mercedes began, "you can afford to eat a few fries." She pointed at Ryann's already tiny figure.

While there may have been some truth to Mercedes' words, Ryann still felt the salad was a better choice.

"How have the treatments been going?" Mackenzie wanted to know.

"I've only had a couple so far. They drain me of all energy and make me feel like not eating so much. When I do force myself to eat, sometimes things just don't taste good."

"I have certainly heard of worse side effects," Angela commented. "Those don't sound too bad."

Ryann nodded her head. "I have been blessed in that regard, at least so far."

Just then Ryann noticed the waitress as she reached around Ryann and put a plate of fresh, steaming French fries in front of her. Ryann looked up at the waitress with a confused look on her face. Before she had a chance to voice her question, Mercedes spoke up.

"Eat the fries if that's what sounds good." She sent a wink in Ryann's direction.

Ryann smiled back. As if to obey her mother, she picked a fry up, making sure Mercedes could see it, and popped it into her mouth, which she quickly regretted because of the temperature, but only for a second.

"Hot!" She waved her hand in front of her open mouth until it cooled a little. Then she took a long drink.

Mercedes winked again. "Just the way you like them."

Ryann took another fry and gingerly took a bite after blowing on it a moment. She tasted hesitantly. After she ate the entire plate of fries she felt better than she had felt in several weeks. And she didn't even feel guilty.

Mercedes

Mercedes knew all too well what it was like to go through chemotherapy. Fortunately, medicine had come quite a ways since her bout with cancer, even though that hadn't been so long ago. One of the things she had learned was to eat what sounded good at the moment. No, not everything that sounded good was the healthiest, but sometimes a body just needed calories. It brought her no small pleasure to spend three dollars on a plate of French fries and watch as her dear friend enjoyed every last one. Mercedes even wondered if Ryann would have licked the plate had she been alone after she ate the last French fry. Mercedes wouldn't have put it past her; neither would Mercedes have blamed her. She'd been there.

Paige

As the group stood from the table to prepare to leave and go their separate ways, Paige noticed the rain.

"Look at that! Good dancing weather!"

"What?" Mercedes asked.

Paige repeated herself. "Good dancing weather."

"I think it's a good stay-inside-curled-up-with-a-book weather." Mackenzie wrinkled up her face as if she were completely disgusted by the rain.

"I agree with Mack," Ryann added her opinion.

"You ladies need to learn to let loose and have a little fun once in a while," Paige said.

"You mean like to dance like no one is watching?" Kayleigh asked.

"Exactly! Don't you remember jumping in mud puddles when you were a kid?"

"I was never a kid."

Paige laughed at Mercedes. "Sure you were. And I bet you knew how to have fun then."

"I'm with Paige. Let's do this."

Before anyone could respond, Angela had made her way out of the restaurant into the rain.

Paige let out a whoop of laughter as she pushed past the others to join Angela. Holding her arms outstretched she lifted her face up to the clouds as she turned in circles. She couldn't help but allow the laughter to bubble up from down deep inside her soul.

It wasn't long before she noticed she and Angela were not alone in the rain dancing. The others had joined the pair, although not quite as uninhibited. Ryann looked up at the sky and let the rain wash her face. Paige couldn't help but wonder if Ryann was dreaming and praying for a miraculous cleansing.

Kayleigh held her hands out as if praying at the same time she was catching raindrops.

Mackenzie was laughing hysterically. Paige laughed when Mack jumped in a puddle. Paige had a feeling there would be more puddle jumping with Mackenzie's boys as soon as the opportunity arose.

Zena was also laughing hysterically. Paige watched as Zena grabbed Mackenzie's hand and they jumped in a huge puddle together.

Mercedes just stood there with her arms across her chest and her head down as if she was trying to keep from getting wet.

"Come on, stick in the mud." Paige grabbed Mercedes' hands and pulled her in a circle like two little girls playing Ring around the Rosie.

"I'm going to regret this. People might see me," Mercedes griped.

"Maybe, but you might regret not doing it even more. No one is promised tomorrow. If you don't dance in the rain today, it might be too late."

"Did you read that on a blog?"

"Maybe."

It wasn't long before even Mercedes was giggling like a schoolgirl. Paige was afraid Mercedes would be upset when she stepped into a puddle that was deep enough to cover her entire foot, but she only laughed harder.

Finally, they all decided it was time to be grown-ups again and ran to their cars. Paige fell into her car, out of breath. She leaned her head back on the headrest, water running down her face. She let out a sigh of pleasure.

"That was fun!"

Mackenzie

Mackenzie was just about at her wit's end. She had spent a couple of hours the previous night crying. Cameron had spent a good share of his evening crying. "Knee hurt!" Was all he kept saying.

At two years old, he still didn't say a lot. She knew his knee hurt, but she couldn't see anything. No bruising or scratches. No red marks. Was it his joints? Did two-year-olds have joint problems?

Big brother was the one who saved the evening. Jordan had been able to distract Cameron by bringing out some old toys. While Cameron had settled some, Mackenzie noticed him slapping his other leg every once in a while. She wondered what was up with that. A day didn't go by that she didn't wish Cameron had a little better vocabulary and could communicate what he was really feeling.

Cameron had screamed like he was in horrendous pain when Mackenzie put on his pajamas. Once settled in bed, he seemed to calm down.

After the boys had fallen asleep Mackenzie could not keep the tears from flowing.

A random thought suddenly came to her mind. Maybe she needed to quit teaching her ladies Bible study at church. That would be one thing off her plate, and she could spend more time with the boys. She grabbed her phone to send a text to Angela. Angela had been there all along and was perfectly capable of taking over the Bible study.

Want to take over Bible study for me?
This week?
Forever.
Why?
It's one thing I can eliminate from my life right now.

Instead of receiving another text, Mackenzie's phone rang. She sighed, not wanting to actually talk to Angela. She thought texting would be enough. She should've known better.

"Hey."

133

"You've been crying, Mack. What's wrong?"

When Mackenzie didn't answer immediately she heard Angela say, "I'll be there in five minutes."

It only seemed like it had been a minute before Angela let herself in and was sitting on the couch, a pint of death by chocolate ice cream sitting between them.

Angela handed Mackenzie a spoon then removed the lid from the carton of ice cream. "Okay. Start talking."

"You're not helping with my diet," Mackenzie gestured toward the ice cream with her spoon.

Angela waved her off. "I'm more concerned about other things right now. What's got you so upset?"

Mackenzie took a deep breath and let it out in a huff. "Besides Cameron?"

Angela bobbed her head back and forth. "I know that's enough, but I feel like there's something more. Why do you want to give up teaching Bible study? You do such an amazing job."

Mackenzie gave in to the ice cream and took a big bite before answering. "I don't know. I guess it would just be one less thing I had to do. I'm feeling a little stressed and overwhelmed."

"I get that," Angela responded. "But can I tell you something?"

"Of course." Mackenzie fed herself another spoonful of the cold creaminess.

"You know I have a lot of connections in missions."

Mackenzie nodded her head as another bite of ice cream passed her lips.

"I've learned something over the years. Those who have a ministry of any sort are often the objects of Satan's attacks. If someone is reaching people with the Gospel of Christ and helping others grow spiritually, they are on Satan's radar. I've seen it way too many times to think it's anything else. Those people who stay in ministry in spite of Satan's attacks do so because they are strong and put their complete faith and trust in God."

Mackenzie was crying again. "But I'm not that strong. And why attack Cameron instead of me? I'm the one with the Bible study."

Angela took Mackenzie's face in her hands, forcing Mackenzie to look at her. "Because if Satan was only attacking you, it wouldn't bother you so much. You probably wouldn't even consider it an issue. But attack your beloved son, and now you have a different story."

Mackenzie thought about Angela's words. Mackenzie knew Angela was right, but that didn't make things any easier.

"But Cameron is just a little boy."

Angela shook her head. "Satan doesn't care. He's doing what he has to do to get to you."

"It's working." Mackenzie grabbed a tissue and gave an unladylike blow. "I don't know what to do."

"I don't want you to give up Bible study. You are doing an amazing job with it, and people are learning a great deal because of it. But if maybe we worked together a little more? We could take turns leading the discussion or something like that."

Mackenzie tilted her head to one side. "That might help. At least a little bit."

Angela patted Mackenzie on the hand. "I'll make sure to pray for you and the boys more. I know how to pray more specifically now."

"Thanks, Angela." Mackenzie was feeling somewhat better. She wasn't sure if it was due to the tears she cried, the true friendship she shared with Angela, or the pint of ice cream she was just now polishing off. Maybe it was a combination of the three.

Angela stood and Mackenzie followed her to the door.

"I am always here if you ever need anything," Angela said, giving Mackenzie a hug.

Mackenzie squeezed Angela back. "I know. There aren't words to express how much I appreciate that."

Ryann

Waiting had never been one of Ryann's strongest characteristics, but this was borderline torturous. She'd had some tests and was waiting for the doctor to come in and give her the results.

"What is taking so long?" Apparently, Mercedes' patience was wearing thin as well.

Ryann giggled. "And I thought it was just me that was going crazy."

"You should be going crazy. You're the patient, and it's normal. But the length of time the doctor has kept us waiting is ridiculous."

Dr. Bernard chose that moment to walk into the room. "I apologize for making you wait so long, but I wanted to consult with some of my colleagues before speaking with you."

Ryann could feel her heart begin beating out of her chest and her face turn hot. Nervousness overtook her. "Is something wrong?" She was barely able to push the words out.

The expression on Dr. Bernard's face was not helping ease Ryann's nerves.

"I don't think so?" He phrased it like a question, which didn't exactly answer Ryann's question.

"What's the issue?"

Ryann could always count on Mercedes to cut to the chase.

"I can't see the tumor anymore," was all Dr. Bernard said.

There was a heavy pause hanging in the room as both Ryann and Mercedes waited for a more thorough explanation, which he wasn't too fast in giving. For someone who was supposed to be a competent doctor, he wasn't living up to that reputation.

"And…" Mercedes drew the word out.

Dr. Bernard just stood there shaking his head. "I've never seen anything like this before. That's why I called you back for the second scan. There was a definite tumor on your very first one, now there's nothing. I had my fellow oncologists look at all the scans and look over your charts. They all are just as baffled as I am. Yes, the tumor should have shrunk, but there is no evidence the tumor had ever been there at all."

Ryann didn't know what to say at first. Mercedes sat completely silent, yet with her mouth open.

"It was God." Ryann broke the silence.

Mercedes turned her head to look at Ryann, mouth still hanging open. Ryann could tell Mercedes finally understood because her mouth closed into a smile and realization broke out across her face.

"Yes," Mercedes concurred. "It was God." She grabbed Ryann's hand and held it tightly.

Dr. Bernard looked at Ryann. "I too believe it was God, and I'll never tire of being able to share these kinds of stories with my unsaved colleagues."

Ryann laughed out loud, wishing she could have seen the looks on the faces of those who only believed in science and never in miracles.

"I want you to come back for one more treatment just to be on the safe side. I'm also going to have you come back regularly for checkups and new scans. When I continue to find nothing it will make your healing all the sweeter."

Ryann couldn't argue with that.

Mackenzie

The house was quiet. Mackenzie had closed her bedroom door, hoping not to wake the boys with what seemed like loud wailing. She tried to keep her sobbing to a dull roar as she poured her heart out to God.

"I can't do this anymore, Lord! I am at my wit's end. I'm exhausted. I'm discouraged. I'm depressed. I'm heartbroken. I've reached the limit of what I can take, even with You by my side. I don't want to see Cameron suffering anymore. Please show me how I can help him. I'm going to take Psalm 5:1-3 literally. 'Listen to my words, LORD, consider my lament. Hear my cry for help, my King and my God, for to you I pray. In the morning, LORD, you hear my voice; in the morning I lay my requests before you and wait expectantly.' I'm going to come before You every day until You answer my prayers."

Pausing a moment to catch her breath and try to organize her thoughts and feelings into some semblance of order, a thought popped into her head. It was a thought she wanted to ignore, but even as she tried to push it away, it wouldn't leave.

She sobbed some more. "God, I don't know if I can call my parents. They hurt me deeply, and that is not something I want for my boys. They've already been through enough."

But then again, she was desperate, and desperate times called for desperate measures, right? It wasn't going to be much longer before they would be living in the car. Then where would they be?

"All right, I'll call them. But only as a last resort. If I can come up with another idea, I'm going with that one first."

After another moment she added, "Forgive my attitude, Lord."

Chapter 9

Not looking to your own interests but each of you to the interests of the others. - Philippians 2:4

May

Angela

Miniature golf. That's what Tom had chosen to do this evening. Angela felt like she was back in high school hanging out with a bunch of friends, including a boy whose attention she had hoped to catch. That boy never even gave her a second glance, but it didn't seem to matter now. Tom was giving her plenty of his attention. Every time he looked at her with his dark brown eyes, Angela took a hold with her own eyes and never wanted to let go. She had to admit she was definitely feeling something for Tom. It had grown to something more than a schoolgirl infatuation. If Tom's glances at her were any indication, his feelings were growing deeper as well.

"Your turn."

Tom's voice brought her attention back to the course. Angela knelt down and placed her ball on the guide hole she thought best lined up with the hole she was attempting to hit her ball into. A nervous laugh erupted out of her when she putted and missed the hole completely.

"I used to be good at this game."

Tom let out a much more conservative laugh. "You just need to warm up."

It didn't take long for Angela to loosen up a little bit more and allow her competitive side to show. Tom reacted with a little friendly competition of his own. "Loser buys milkshakes."

"You're on."

The couple teased and cajoled each other the remainder of the eighteen holes. The score was neck and neck. In the end, Angela lost by one stroke.

"I guess milkshakes are on me."

However, upon ordering, Tom pushed her away from the card reader with his hip. Angela stumbled a couple of steps to the side before she was able to insert her debit card.

"What are you doing?"

"I wouldn't be much of a gentleman if I let you pay."

"But I lost fair and square."

"You can get the next ones." He made his statement while looking pointedly at Angela.

She found herself holding onto his brown eyes again. Was he saying something more? *Oh, I hope so!* she thought to herself. Then in a moment of composure, *Lord, don't let me get ahead of You.*

Ryann

Ryann woke up with a smile. Yes, she had to go to the hospital to have her treatment today; however, this was the last time she would have to go. After today, her body could rest and return to normal.

"You awake, Mom?" Jocelyn quietly knocked on the bedroom door.

"I'm awake."

"But you need to be getting out of bed," Jocelyn teased.

"I'm working on it," Ryann fussed playfully. Throwing back the covers she added, "I'm actually looking forward to getting out of bed today, even for that blasted treatment."

Then she took a moment to really look at her daughter. She turned her head slightly and narrowed her eyes. "What do you have up your sleeve, Jocelyn?"

Jocelyn shrugged her shoulders, "I don't know what you're talking about. I guess I'm just happy about today as well."

Ryann kept an eye on Jocelyn as she picked out comfortable clothes for Ryann to put on after she got out of the shower. Ryann was sure her daughter was planning something. She could tell Jocelyn was trying not to smile.

When Jocelyn turned from the closet, Ryann caught her eyes. At first, Jocelyn immediately acted like she had as a child when she had been caught in some form of mischief. But then she turned to her mother by putting her hands on her hips and threatening Ryann with the same statement she herself had often used on the girls.

"Are you going to get in the shower or am I going to have to drag you in there myself?"

Ryann threw a pillow at her. "I'm going. I'm going."

As Ryann showered, she was grateful there wouldn't be any more of these early morning visits. She was not a fan of mornings anyway; this whole cancer situation had not changed her mind on that one bit.

Later, when they arrived at the treatment room at the hospital, she discovered why Jocelyn had been so smiley. The room had been decorated in her favorite colors and all of the lunch ladies were there.

"Happy graduation day!" they shouted in unison.

Ryann could not help but smile. Tears came to her eyes as her friends came up to hug her.

"We're staying with you for your entire LAST treatment." Zena placed all of her Greek accented emphasis on the word "last."

"I brought something for you." Kayleigh handed her a small box that tinkled a bit as Ryann unwrapped it.

Ryann pulled out a little bell.

"I know they have a bell here you can ring after your last treatment, but I thought you might like a reminder to take home to show how far God has brought you and how He has never left your side."

Now Ryann's tears were really flowing. She couldn't say a word. She wrapped Kayleigh in a huge hug and squeezed as hard as she could.

"You're squeezing the stuffing right out of me," Kayleigh eventually gasped.

Ryann laughed as she let go. "Sorry!"

"Are we ready to get this party started?" Dr. Bernard entered and asked.

"Started and finished," Ryann said, taking her normal seat.

Throughout her treatment, the lunch ladies sang, laughed, and prayed. Other patients who were also having treatments often joined in. The lunch ladies, true to form, took time to greet the other patients individually. Ryann drifted away from the conversation around her as Kayleigh, with her pen and little black book in hand, took the time with each person in the room to write down prayer requests and pray.

A tear rolled down Ryann's cheek. She didn't even notice it until Mackenzie took a tissue from her purse and wiped it away.

"Don't worry," she said. "It's almost over."

Ryann shook her head and sniffed. "It's not that."

"What is it?" Paige asked.

Ryann smiled. "It's you guys. There are no better friends."

It only took a moment before Mackenzie was swiping at tears of her own and Paige was sniffling.

Finally, the treatment was completed, the bell rung, and Ryann allowed to leave with an "I-hope-to-never-see-you-again" from Doctor Bernard along with the comment, "I have truly never seen any patient like you before. I don't know how the tumor shrunk so much from one scan to the next without having any treatments of any kind. I know you have friends in high places. I do have to say, though, we should have allowed your friends to come in all together sooner. I've never felt a higher morale in this room. You lifted a lot of people's spirits today and given them hope for the future."

Ryann knew without a shadow of a doubt it was her friends' faithful prayers for her that had healing powers. From their lips to God's ears to Ryann's body.

∞ ∞ ∞

Paige

At lunch, Paige made what she felt was a bold and exciting announcement.

"I'm going to start a blog."

"Really?" Mercedes asked.

"Yes. I already read a lot of blogs, so I know what people are interested in. I used to like to write when I was a little girl. I would write stories about big families."

"I never knew that about you." Ryann's smile encouraged Paige.

"I also know a lot of bloggers make money with advertising. A little extra cash couldn't hurt."

"Don't be surprised if it takes a while to build an audience and start making that money."

Paige knew Mercedes had a head for business and took her words to heart. She did not want to start something only to quit soon after out of disappointment.

"I realize that," she responded.

"What can we do to help?" Kayleigh asked.

"Well, when I get it all ready you can follow me. It would also help if you read my posts and then commented on them. The more traffic I have the better."

"We'll all be sure to do just that," Zena said. "What are you going to write about?"

This was something Paige had put the most thought into. "Dating, blind dating, setting people up."

"That definitely sounds interesting," Angela said.

Mackenzie

"How has Cameron been feeling, Mack? Any changes?" Kayleigh leaned over and asked.

Mackenzie shook her head. "No, no changes, at least not ones for the better. The doctors are putting him through a bunch of tests. In some ways, I think the tests are worse than the issues he's been dealing with. They're almost torture. It's torture for me to have to watch him go through them."

"I can't imagine what you're going through. I'll continue to pray…for both of you."

"Thanks, Kayleigh. I don't think you realize how much your prayers mean to me." Mackenzie would ever be grateful for friends like Kayleigh. She thought about asking Kayleigh to pray for something else, but she didn't really want anyone else to hear. She wasn't sure she wanted any of her friends to know the thoughts that went through her mind at times.

"Could you pray for something else for me, too?" Mackenzie discreetly leaned over and whispered to Kayleigh.

Kayleigh just as discreetly responded. "Of course."

"It's my attitude. I feel like God is punishing me. I mean, I look back over my life and I wonder why I have had so many more problems than other people seem to have."

"I don't think that's true."

"My heart knows that, I think, but there's no communication between my head and my heart. And my heart is speaking louder right now." Mackenzie sighed.

"Your attitude is understandable. You're under a lot of stress. But be assured that I'll be praying for you, Mack."

"Thanks, Kayleigh."

They went back to eating; at least Kayleigh went back to eating. Mackenzie only picked at her food. There was no better time than the present to make her announcement.

"I have some bad news."

Everyone stopped and looked at her.

"I found a job," Mackenzie stated.

All the ladies began talking at once.

"That's not bad news."

"Congratulations!"

"That's great news."

"It's back in Ohio," she added quietly.

"Wait, what?" Paige asked loud enough for all in the restaurant to hear. "You can't move away!"

All of a sudden, the chatter dissipated.

Mackenzie shrugged her shoulders. "I need a job desperately and nothing seems to be working out here. I keep applying and getting no responses. Work-at-home jobs just don't pay enough. Ohio is where my family is. They can help out with the kids. I want my parents to be able to spend as much time with Cameron as possible."

"Before he dies?"

The ladies all knew exactly what Mackenzie meant, but Paige had to vocalize it, even though it wasn't a sure thing.

Mackenzie didn't miss the look Mercedes shot Paige.

Mercedes put her arm around Mackenzie. "As hard as it's going to be for all of us, we understand that you need to make decisions that are best for your family."

"There's also a little more to it than that."

"Like what, Mack?" Ryann asked.

"I've been contacted by some doctors who want to put Cam in a test group. Maybe they can figure out what's wrong with him. It's all free, and I don't feel as if I have any other choice. All these doors seem to be opening for me to go home, and nothing here is falling into place. I guess this is what God wants for us."

145

But if it was of God, why did she feel so torn? Shouldn't there be peace of some sort in her heart?

Mackenzie sighed. "I don't even know what's really best anymore."

No one made any noise at all for a moment. No silverware hitting the plates. No ice jostling in glasses. No one speaking. Mackenzie wasn't even sure if any of them were still breathing.

But then Ryann broke the silence. "When do you have to leave?"

"Probably within the next month or so. As soon as I can pack up all my stuff." Then she thought to herself, *I'll wait as long as I can possibly drag it out!*

"You are right," Zena started. "This is bad news."

"Is there anything we can help you with?" Angela asked.

"Not really."

"We can all come and help you pack," Paige said.

Mackenzie knew Paige meant well, but it still sounded odd. Mackenzie realized it must've sounded the same to Mercedes when she said, "We'll all come. We'll order pizza and have a grand old time."

"I'll be there. I'll bring some of my kids to play with the boys. That will be a help."

"Right." Mackenzie felt that the smile on her face was as far from real as it could get. She was not going to enjoy leaving her friends. "Can we just change the subject now? I don't want to spoil our lunch, and I don't want to think about what I'll be missing."

Zena

It was the last day of the homeschool co-op for the year. As much as she loved the camaraderie with other homeschool moms, her children spending the day with friends, and teaching her classes, she was ready for a break. Shaking her head and trying to find the energy to get through the day, she couldn't help but wonder how some families schooled all year around. She knew she needed that summer break.

Besides, her garden was beginning to produce, and that was what she wanted to spend her time on now. There was really nothing better than seeing all the shelves in the basement full of the fruits of her labor. Because of so much overabundance of veggies and fruit last year, she had been able to share a lot, especially with Mackenzie and the boys.

At the thought of Mackenzie, Zena remembered that Mackenzie was leaving soon. It just about broke her heart. Not just for herself but for Mackenzie also. Zena was pretty sure Mackenzie did not want to leave. If she did, she would have seemed happier about it.

Lord, if there is anything I can do to make Mack and the boys stay here, please show me.

She didn't have the time for more prayer than that as the students for her last class of the day began entering the room.

"Oh, thank you!" she said to one of her students who handed her a card and a canning jar full of chocolates.

Other students gave her precious notes and gifts. She had to keep herself from laughing when several of the boys literally tossed a card her way with the simple, "Here." While the girls were all full of hugs and even some tears, the boys were shy to show any emotion. All of these fourth and fifth graders were special to her.

"Did you bring your completed projects?" Zena had to shout to get their attention.

Several students held their projects up in the air as an answer, but the talking did not diminish at all.

"Can I get everyone's attention, please? Woohoo. Look up here." She raised one hand hoping the motion would catch their eyes, but it didn't.

Zena let out a heavy sigh and looked down at her one student that was paying attention. "Herding cats, Lola. That's what I'm attempting to do here!"

Lola giggled.

Zena winked at her and said, "Plug your ears."

Lola quickly obeyed as Zena put two fingers in her mouth and let out a piercing whistle. It was her special whistle she used to call her children into the house when they were out roaming the farm. It also succeeded in getting her students' attention as the echoes of the sound slammed from one cinderblock wall of the room to the other.

"That's better."

But before she could say anything to her finally settled class, someone knocked on the door and poked her head in.

"Have you seen Amanda?" the worried mother wanted to know.

Zena stepped over to the door to hear better as she had lost control of her class once again. "No. She isn't in my class."

"Someone saw a strange man in the parking lot earlier, and I haven't seen Amanda for the last hour. Normally I wouldn't worry about her since she's usually with friends, but the ones I've caught up with don't know where she is."

Zena turned to her students and shouted, "Don't make me whistle again," to which the room settled quickly. "Have any of you seen Amanda?"

Those who did respond did so negatively.

When she closed the door to get back to class, Zena sent up yet another quick prayer. She wished she could be out helping to find Amanda, but she couldn't leave eighteen rambunctious rascals to their own devices either.

What would happen then!

It took another moment to get the students ready to begin sharing their projects. Chaos reigned for the next thirty

148

minutes as one person after another interrupted the class wanting to know if anyone had seen Amanda.

Zena was about ready to call it quits for the day when one of her students tapped her on the arm.

"Miss Zena."

"Yes?"

"I'm sorry." She pointed under a table in the back corner of the room where she and a couple of the other girls had been sitting.

It was then Zena noticed that some strategically placed backpacks hid someone under their table.

Amanda.

Zena's heart had been racing in fear since Amanda's mom had first come to the door. Now it was racing for another reason. She kicked other backpacks out of the way as she scrambled to the back of the room.

"You're coming with me," she said bending down to grab one of Amanda's hands and drag her out from underneath the table.

The group of girls who had hidden her all tried to give Amanda hugs before she left.

"You girls can hug each other later. Right now I'm sure your mom is worried sick about you."

As soon as Zena opened the classroom door, she saw Amanda's mom standing near the end of the hallway.

"Oh!" She ran up to Amanda and grabbed her in a fierce squeeze. "What were you doing? Where were you?"

Deciding to put the incident behind her, Zena went back into her class and closed the door. Leaning against it she closed her eyes and let out a thankful sigh. Amanda was safe. Then she eyeballed the girls in the corner. They were not so safe. School was still in session, and it was time for one more lesson.

Later that evening a barrage of texts started.

Did you have a good day? followed by a wink emoji.

Yes, Zena responded. *Last day of school.*

You didn't get any jail time for harboring fugitives? Another wink emoji followed by some handcuffs.

Now it all made sense. Word of what happened at co-op must have gotten out.

Why do I hang around you people? she asked.

Because you love us.

And we love you.

Did Cooper have enough bail money?

How did you even find out? Zena wondered who been talking.

Ummm… The co-op is a ministry of our church. Did you think we wouldn't find out?

The good-natured ribbing went on for a while longer. She could hear each one of them laughing hysterically at her expense, but she was okay with it. Now that it was over, it was sort of funny. Sort of. Zena knew she would never live this down.

Mercedes

The texts about Zena's day could not have come at a better time. She had been texting Annie, but that conversation had not held one ounce of humor.

I'm texting because I can't even stand to hear your voice. You have always been so judgmental of me. I could never do anything right. You criticized every move I made and you never accepted who I was. I don't know if we can ever have a relationship after this. You've just gone too far.

Mercedes wasn't even sure exactly what she had done. The accusations Annie was throwing at her didn't make sense. Mercedes didn't know for sure but figured Annie was being influenced by ungodly people.

There was one point where Annie had told Mercedes that she was seeing a counselor because Mercedes had been such a horrible mother. While Mercedes had never gone to a counselor herself, she knew they could be very one-sided. The advice some people received was far from good or beneficial to healing broken relationships. Many counselors in the secular world would take the side of their client and say what the client wanted to hear. Which kind of made sense. What counselor would want to tell their client what they needed to hear over what they wanted to hear and risk losing a customer?

After prayer and even some fasting, Mercedes decided to keep her struggles with Annie to herself. If she never said anything to anyone, not even the lunch ladies, she could be sure that what Annie was hearing from wherever definitely did not come from Mercedes' mouth. She had asked Kayleigh to pray for an unspoken request, but that was as far as she would go.

Kayleigh

Kayleigh had some time to herself and decided to pull out her prayer journal. There were so many things on her mind and heart she knew the only way to release them was to write them down in prayer.

Dear precious heavenly Father. I want to come before You tonight with praise and thanksgiving. I thank You that Ryann has finished her treatments. I know she is glad to be through with them. I knew it was Your hand upon her, answering the prayers of Your beloved children, that she did not have to have surgery and more intense treatments. Others may be baffled by her healing, but I'm not. You are a God of miracles, and nothing takes You by surprise.

I want to thank You for answering prayers regarding Mack and her family. Thank You for providing a job for her.

Thank You for opening the door to possibly getting Cameron much needed medical attention.

In the midst of my thanks, there are still so many needs. I pray for Angela and her newfound joy. I don't know what You have in store for her and Tom, but I pray that You lead and guide them in the way You want them to go.

I pray also for Mercedes, God. I don't know why she comes to my mind so often lately, but there must be a reason You continue to nudge me about her. Maybe it's because of her relationship with Annie. I know Mercedes' heart is broken over their falling out, but Lord, even that You can restore.

One by one, Kayleigh went through the names of her friends and prayed specifically for each one of them. Even though she spent well over an hour writing out her prayers in her journal, she felt revived and refreshed after spending precious time with the Lord.

Chapter 10

Carry each other's burdens, and in this way you will fulfill the law of Christ. - Galatians 6:2

June

Angela

Angela sat down at the table next to Paige. She purposely put her hand out so her new jewelry would be obvious. As expected, Paige loudly made a big deal of it.

"What is that?" Paige shouted and pointed at the same time, drawing the attention of everyone else at the table and in the restaurant.

Angela held her hand up in front of her turning it back and forth so everyone could get a good look at it. "Oh, this old thang," she said in her best, exaggerated southern accent.

In unison, the ladies all screamed.

"Congratulations!" was heard several times around the room.

"That was a whirlwind romance if I've ever seen one," said a smiling Zena.

"But we've known each other for years," Angela reminded

"You just never had the sense to start a relationship until I put the two of you together," Paige boasted. "Oh, you know what this means?" She put her hands over her mouth, her eyes wide open.

"I'm getting married?" Angela stated the obvious meaning.

"We're going to be sisters for real!" Paige threw her arms around Angela's neck, just about choking her.

"Yes, yes, we will be sisters," Angela laughed at the same time she was trying to peel Paige off her.

Everyone took turns admiring the ring and giving Angela congratulatory hugs.

As they were all returning to normal and looking at menus, Paige asked, "Aren't you glad I tried to set you up on blind dates?"

"Not all of them!" Angela answered emphatically.

"But I finally found you the right one."

"Yes, you certainly did, Paige."

Angela had to admit, all of the previous setups had been worth it in order to get this point. She couldn't imagine being any happier.

"So, where are you guys going to live?" Kayleigh wondered.

Angela pretended to be concentrating on her menu for a moment before she answered.

"You're leaving us, aren't you?" Ryann asked quietly.

"What?" Paige was louder.

Angela figured it would be best if she just came right out with it. "I'm going to the mission field with Tom."

"You can't! What about me?" Paige was a little overdramatic.

"You get to fulfill your childhood dream of being a missionary," Mercedes commented.

"Yes, I do. We've been talking to the mission board about me joining him. We didn't want to make any marriage decisions or announcements until we were certain it would all work out."

"God pulled all your plans together, didn't He?" Kayleigh stated more than asked a question.

Angela nodded her head. She was still in awe of how God had worked everything out and so quickly, even though it had taken so long to get to this point.

"We'll miss you, but we're so happy for you at the same time," Mackenzie said.

"You'll have to make sure you're not so busy that you can't keep in touch," Zena said firmly.

"I promise I'll call, write, and post on the Internet regularly."

Paige pouted.

"What's wrong?" Angela asked.

Paige answered by looking at Angela. "Did you know that to keep yourself from being lonely, you'll have to come and visit us face to face? The more time we spend on the Internet together, the lonelier you'll be."

"I don't know where you get your information from," Ryann commented.

"I read blogs." The way Paige said it, made it sound like it should be common knowledge.

Zena shook her head. "You have too much time on your hands.

"So, when's the wedding?" Zena wondered, taking the opportunity to change the subject.

"The end of the month."

"That's only three weeks!" Paige could not contain herself.

"And when do you leave?"

Angela paused for a moment, knowing no one would be happy with the response. "The same day. And before any of you say anything, I want you to know our decisions were not made hastily. We put every decision before God, including this one."

She then turned and looked at Mackenzie. "Mack, I know things have been hard for you lately. We want you to take the boys and come and live in my house rent-free."

Mackenzie had a blank look on her face as if she hadn't heard or didn't understand what Angela was saying.

"What?" she whispered.

"I know you will still need to find work, but maybe it will help you stay here where you're loved. We want you to live in my house rent-free. I don't want to sell it because we want someplace to stay when we come home to visit, that's the one condition. You have to let us stay there whenever we come home. The house is huge and would be wasted if it just sat empty."

Angela paused as Mackenzie wiped a tear from her eye.

"We thought it would help you out financially, and the boys could make use of the backyard."

"I don't know what to say." Mackenzie looked dumbfounded.

"I say we move the moving party to Angela's house, and we can kill two birds with one stone; get her ready to leave and you ready to come," Kayleigh said.

"I think that's a great idea," Angela smiled at Mackenzie who still couldn't seem to find the words to say.

Angela took a hold of Mackenzie's hand.

"Thank you!" Mackenzie's words were barely audible, but Angela got the message.

Ryann

Life certainly was a roller coaster. Ryann felt a little dizzy trying to keep up with all of it.

Mackenzie and the boys were leaving.

Angela was getting married.

She and Tom would be leaving.

Mackenzie was back to not leaving.

Ryann's heart didn't know what to feel.

"Well," Ryann began, trying to make sense of everything that was happening, "You need to let us help you prepare for the wedding, Angela."

Angela waved her hand. "Oh, I don't need anything big."

"You do need food," Zena said. "And I'll take care of all that. You just let me know how many people are coming."

156

Ryann pulled an old grocery receipt and a pen from her purse and began taking notes on the back.

"Put me down for decorations," Mackenzie offered.

"I told you I didn't want to make a big deal out of all this," Angela said.

"You aren't," Ryann finished what she was writing down and looked up to meet Angela's eyes. "We are." She opened her eyes wide and wiggled her eyebrows.

"Don't spoil our excitement!" Paige said. "What do you need me to do?" Paige directed her question to Ryann.

"I'll take care of the guestbook and prayer cards so people can remember to pray for your marriage and your ministry. They will make great favors."

Ryann smiled at Kayleigh for coming up with the perfect addition to the wedding preparations that had her fingerprints all over it. Ryann added Kayleigh's idea to the list.

"I guess I'm the only one that doesn't have a job," Mercedes said.

"You can help me; we will be the gophers. We'll help everyone else with whatever they're working on," Paige responded.

Mercedes smiled. "That sounds like a plan. I think our first order of business is to help Angela pick out a dress."

"Oh!" Ryann burst out. "We should all go!" Some memories of shopping for her own wedding dress popped into her head

Angela held up her hands. "Wait, wait, wait!" she began. "You ladies don't need to go bat crazy. A simple wedding is all we want. A simple dress. A simple menu–"

"Simply beautiful." Ryann interrupted, took hold of Angela's hand, and squeezed. She looked directly at Angela and pleaded with her eyes. For good measure she added, "Besides this may be one of the last things I get to plan, being so sick and all."

"Oh, stop it," Angela gasped. "You're fine. The doctor said so!"

"Ryann is being a little overdramatic," Mercedes rolled her eyes. "But we all feel the same way about wanting to have a hand in the day you've waited for for so long. We just want it to be perfect for you."

Angela sighed and looked down at the table. "You guys are ridiculous," she stated. "On the other hand, you're the best group of friends a girl could ask for."

A chorus of cheers rose from the ladies as they all gathered around Angela with more hugs.

Zena

Before the lunchtime ended, Zena had a proposition to make. "Could we meet for lunch at a park next month? Cooper will be out of town, and I won't have anyone to watch the kids for me. If we went to a park, I could bring them and still spend time with you."

"Sounds like a good idea to me," Ryann said. "Anyone have a problem with it?"

"What if it's a fiasco like when we changed restaurants?" Paige wondered.

Mercedes looked to her with her face all scrunched up. "What kind of food fiasco would happen at the park? Bring your own picnic lunch and you're all set to go."

Paige looked to Mercedes and said, "Oh."

Ryann rolled her eyes before suggesting a park that had a great playground for kids before they all went their separate ways.

Mackenzie

It didn't take long for Mackenzie to pack up all their belongings. Stuff had never been important to her even as a child. She wondered now if that had been God's way of preparing her for a life devoid of "stuff." Mackenzie was perfectly fine with it.

She was glad she had most everything packed before the lunch ladies came over. They seemed intent on doing more fooling around than working. Mackenzie blamed her frustrated feelings on her excitement to be out of the dingy rental house, so she tried to keep her feelings under control.

Finally, Zena's van was all packed. Zena had offered the use of her fifteen-passenger van. With the seats taken out, there was ample room for all of Mackenzie's and the boys' belongings. It was almost embarrassing. But then she began counting her blessings. If all of God's blessings were tangible, there was no way they would have all fit in the van. She knew that when this life came to an end, how many dishes she had managed to accumulate wouldn't matter. The real blessings would still be with her.

When all was packed, Mackenzie led the caravan to Angela's house. As she pulled into the driveway, she noticed the caravan was not behind her. Since she figured the rest of the ladies would be along shortly, she took the opportunity to go into the house by herself.

Angela threw the door opened and stepped out on the porch to welcome Mackenzie with open arms.

On the verge of tears...again, Mackenzie said, "Thanks so much for doing this for us."

Angela acted as if it were nothing. "Thank you for being willing to take care of my home."

As Mackenzie looked around, she realized how clean the house was. She envisioned her boys tracking in mud and breaking things.

"It's so clean."

"It's so empty."

Mackenzie quickly twisted her head to look Angela in the eye. There was no mistaking her meaning. The house was perfect because there were no children to enjoy it. Mackenzie smiled at her friend. "It won't be anymore."

"I can't wait."

Mackenzie knew Angela meant it. While Angela had accumulated more possessions over the years than Mackenzie had, Angela also valued the spiritual over the temporal.

Their moment was broken by the arrival of the caravan.

"We stopped for the pizza." Paige held several boxes in front of her chest. "Where do you want them, Angela?"

"Come this way."

As Angela led Paige out of the room, Mackenzie took one more look around her. Yes, her life was definitely looking up.

Mackenzie

"Knock, knock," Mackenzie said as she poked her head in the door of the bridal room where Angela was preparing for the ceremony.

"Oh, Mack! Please, come in."

Mackenzie couldn't help but notice Angela's face; its brilliant beauty surpassed the dress by miles. "Your face shows how happy you are."

Angela held her hands up to either side of her face.

"I like it," Mackenzie said.

"I guess I just waited so long, I can't believe it's actually going to happen."

Mackenzie pulled her surprise out from behind her back and held it out. "A special bouquet for a special bride."

"Oh, Mack, it's absolutely gorgeous!" Angela buried her face in it and took a deep breath. "It smells so good!"

"I did a little research–"

"Of course you did," Angela interrupted.

Mackenzie smiled. "This is a traditional wedding bouquet. They used to have meaning, not just be a coordinating accessory." She pointed to each flower or herb as she mentioned them. "The day lily is white and stands for purity and innocence. The violet stands for faithfulness. The thyme for grace and elegance. The tansy for the immortality of your love for each other. The sage is a reminder to esteem each other and lift each other up. Rosemary symbolizes loyalty, friendship, and long-lasting love. Mint represents the joy of new love. Marjoram stands for beauty. Lemon balm gives healing when there's discord. Ivy represents fidelity, and the fern symbolizes sincerity. This branch of Dogwood proves you can weather any storm that comes your way. These are all things I wish for you and Tom today and in the years to come."

Angela didn't say anything right away. She took a deep breath and fanned her hand in front of her face. "You're making me cry, and I'm trying not to cry and ruin my makeup." After one more breath, she was able to say, "What a beautiful and thoughtful gift. I will treasure it forever."

Mackenzie gave Angela a hug. "It's almost time. I'll come get you when we're ready." She winked as she left the room.

Zena

"Don't even breathe," Zena demanded when she sensed Mackenzie, Paige, and Mercedes coming up behind her.

She very carefully placed the final layer on the top of the cake. Grabbing the bag of frosting from the right side of the table, she added some finishing touches of piping around where the layers met. She stood back to examine her work. Squinting, she tilted her head to view her wedding cake creation from a different point of view. Turning and noticing Mackenzie had some flowers in her hands, she asked, "Are you doing anything with those?"

Mackenzie shook her head and held out the bunch of flowers.

Apparently, Mackenzie was waiting for Zena's permission to speak. But Zena wasn't ready for conversation yet; she was still concentrating on her work. She took one of Mack's flowers and popped the blooms off the stems. She strategically placed the fresh blooms around the layers of the cake.

Once again, she stepped back to examine her work. "Perfect," she smiled. Then she remembered those who were standing behind her. "Okay. You can speak now."

"Zena, that's beautiful!"

"Wow!"

"You have definitely outdone yourself," Mercedes put her arm around Zena's shoulders.

"And it tastes as good as it looks!" Paige had picked up the bag of leftover frosting, squeezed a bit out onto her finger, and put it in her mouth. "Here, try some." She squeezed frosting out onto Mackenzie's finger.

"Oh, that's delicious!" Mackenzie agreed.

Zena then turned around and got a view of how the other three had transformed the Fellowship Hall of the church into a perfectly beautiful dream wedding reception.

"Look what you have done!" she exclaimed. "Angela is going to be so pleased."

"Is everyone ready?" Ryann entered the room, and then abruptly stopped. She looked around at all the decorating details, as well as at Zena's cake. "You have certainly left your marks here. Angela is going to love it."

"I hope so," Zena said, giving her cake one last look. The perfectionist in her still wasn't quite pleased.

Kayleigh

"Come on, girls, we're about to have a wedding," Kayleigh called from the doorway. "There's an empty pew up at the front of the church waiting for us to fill it."

The five of them scurried out of the Fellowship Hall and headed to the sanctuary. Kayleigh sat on the end of the pew, furthest away from the aisle. She had been on the verge of tears all day. All the time they had spent arranging things for Angela's wedding, Kayleigh could not help but think back to her own wedding day. It had been a fairytale of a day. However, the fairytale had been short-lived. At least once Angela made her walk to the front of the church where Tom stood waiting to make her his bride, Kayleigh could let her tears flow and no one would be the wiser. She certainly did not want to ruin Angela's special day with her sad tears of what she had once hoped for in a loving husband.

Yes, he had gone to church a couple of times, but he hadn't quite turned his life over to the Lord just yet.

With her eyes open and on her gorgeous friend, she prayed. *Lord, bring him back to You. Help him to also find his way back to me as the man of my dreams. I put him in Your hands. Amen.*

Even though it took great effort, Kayleigh forced herself to focus on the new couple.

Paige

Paige's face felt like it was going to break. It hurt from smiling so much, but she couldn't help it, and she didn't want to help it. She could not remember a day ever before in her life when she had been so happy.

Her life had never been normal compared to other people's, whatever normal was, and she always dreamed about having siblings. As a child, she had decided she was going to have several children of her own when she got married one day, that way her children would never be without playmates, and she would never be lonely.

There may not have been a man in her life at the moment, but she had a good start on her family. Her brother had gone out of his way to find her. And now that brother was marrying one of her best friends.

Angela

This was really happening. Angela felt as if she was having an out of body experience. She kept waiting to wake up from a dream–the best dream ever! The day was a whirlwind of activity. Every moment she was grateful to the group of women who surrounded her. No, at first she had not wanted to make a big deal of the wedding, but a marriage was a big deal. Marriage was a gift from God, a gift that God had finally blessed her with. She knew God's timing was always perfect. While there were times she may have doubted His timing in the past, she vowed to never doubt Him again.

Smiling, she looked at Tom, her husband. That word was new and exciting at the same time. She wondered what God had in store for their future.

Mercedes

When Mercedes arrived home later that evening after the wedding, she flopped down in her comfy chair. She was exhausted, but every aching muscle was worth it. She knew she would have to start eliminating things from her schedule. She just couldn't do everything anymore. But, she wouldn't have missed today for anything in the world. Angela had been the most beautiful bride she had ever seen. Mercedes was so happy for Tom and Angela. If only things in her own life were so perfect.

She shook her head. She was not going to dwell on the negative. Life was too short for that. Instead, she relived each moment of the day. First seeing Angela all dressed up. The look on Tom's face when he got his first glimpse of his bride. The music. The food. The dancing. The laughter. The celebrating.

Mercedes fell asleep right there in her chair with a contented smile on her face.

Chapter 11

For where two or three gather in my name, there am I with them. - Matthew 18:20

July

Ryann

"Everything still looks great." Dr. Bernard said, shoving some papers into a file.

Ryann finally allowed herself to breathe. She hadn't realized how nervous she had been for her follow-up appointment. Of course, she wasn't sure how much change there would be in a month or two. The thought that the doctors could have been wrong about her diagnosis all along or that they had been looking at another person's records by mistake, a person who was healthy while Ryann was not.

Placing the folder on the desk, Dr. Bernard interrupted her thoughts. "I guess I'll see you in six months. You can make that appointment on your way out."

"Are you sure everything is okay?" There was still a part of Ryann that didn't believe God could work a miracle in her. Not that she didn't believe in miracles, but that God loved her that much.

Dr. Bernard smiled at her. "If anything feels strange or different or even just uncomfortable, give me a call and I'll get you in."

"Thank you." Ryann felt silly because of her worries. "Thank you for everything."

He gave her a wink. "See you in six months."

$$\infty \quad \infty \quad \infty$$

Paige

Paige knew she was running really late, but she didn't care. Not that she ever cared she was always late, but this time there was a good reason. It was lunch day and Angela had said she would send them a letter before then. Paige had seen her mailman walking up the street that intersected with hers and knew he would be there shortly.

"What is taking him so long?" she wondered aloud.

Then she figured if she waited outside he wouldn't even have to walk all the way up the sidewalk and steps to get to her mailbox. She grabbed her purse and keys and decided to wait by the car.

Finally, she saw him walking in her direction.

"Hey!" Paige called out to him. "If you have anything for me, I'll take it and save you a few steps."

"Great. Thanks," he said as he handed her a few envelopes.

As she sat in her car, Paige sorted through all the junk mail, throwing it on the floor of the passenger side.

"I don't want any of this," she fussed at the credit card applications that seemed to come daily. "I don't want this either," she said to the bills for the credit cards she did have.

There. The special looking envelope with Angela's handwriting. "This I want."

She placed the letter with her purse. She would wait to open it until they were all together.

Mackenzie

Mackenzie came running to where the rest of the ladies had started setting up their picnic lunches. She was sure she looked rather comical carrying a picnic basket, Cameron, and fussing at Jordan behind her. She figured they would have fun playing with Zena's kids.

"You guys will never guess what happened!"

At first, everyone just stared at her in shock. No one had ever heard her speak so loudly or so excitedly before.

Everyone's lack of enthusiasm left Mackenzie feeling a little disappointed. "Isn't anyone going to guess?"

"Why don't you tell us? I'm sure we would probably never guess right anyway," Ryann encouraged her.

Still bouncing off the walls, Mackenzie nodded her head. "You're right. You will never guess. I had a greeting card company contact me. They offered me a job designing a line of cards for them. It means I can stay home with my boys and not have to find a job outside of the house."

"So you'll never have to move?" Ryann asked the question that was now on everyone's mind.

Mackenzie nodded her head vigorously. With the job and living in Angela's house rent-free, she would be able to take care of her boys. She couldn't remember the last time she'd been so happy.

All of a sudden there was complete chaos. There was lots of cheering, hugging, and screaming.

"How did this happen? Zena wondered.

Mackenzie looked to Kayleigh and smiled. "Kayleigh made a comment at Christmas time that I should sell them. That got me thinking and I did a little research. I took a shot in the dark. I figured the worst they could say was no and I'd be no worse off than I am now. I contacted them a while ago and they are just now getting back to me."

"They're paying you for this?" Kayleigh wanted to make sure it wasn't a scam.

"Yes. It's not a ton of money, but enough to take care of us. I'm so happy! I did not want to leave you ladies, and I really did not want to go home. I know my parents wanted us there, but they didn't want us there for the right reasons."

"We're so happy for you, Mack," Ryann gave her friend's hand a squeeze.

"What about the test group Cameron was going to be a part of?" Kayleigh wondered.

Mackenzie smiled even bigger, if that were possible. "God worked that out as well. When I called to tell them our plans had changed and that we would not be coming after all, they were still interested in Cameron. They set us up with a specialist here."

"Wonderful!" Kayleigh's smile matched Mackenzie's.

"I'm happy you're not leaving. I know it's a little selfish on my part, but it's the truth." Kayleigh put her arms around Mackenzie in a bear hug. "We're your family, too. We'll all help you take care of those precious boys."

Everyone agreed to Kayleigh's last statement which brought tears to Mackenzie's eyes. Oh, how could she have ever thought of leaving these dear ladies? Kayleigh was right; they were her family

As much as she hated to admit it, Mackenzie knew exactly what it would have been like had she gone home. All three of them would have been crammed into a teeny tiny room. They would never have had any time to themselves as her parents would always be hovering since she wasn't a decent mom and all. Not to mention the judgmental potshots they would constantly aim at Mackenzie for all the "wrong" decisions she had made. She also had no reason to believe her parents would treat their grandsons any differently than they treated her growing up. The thought had occurred to her on more than one occasion that she had married "that man" as a way to get out from underneath the thumbs of her parents, but then there was his thumb. She definitely did not want her precious boys subjected to that.

If her parents had really wanted to be involved in the boys' lives, they could have come for visits. Or at least sent cards on their birthdays. Or called once a while. Or... No,

Mackenzie had to stop that line of thinking. Nothing good would come of it, and nothing would change.

How hard she had been praying for God to open the door so she wouldn't have to move away from here. She found much more support here with her friends. Her true family. She was just sad that Angela had walked through that open door in the opposite direction.

Paige

When Paige finally arrived at the park, she just about ran to where everyone else was gathered around Mackenzie. Paige waved the envelope over her head as she stumbled on the uneven ground, almost face planting in the grass.

"Look what I have! I'm late because I was waiting for the mailman, hoping he might bring a word from Tom and Angela today."

"It will be nice when they get settled and can get Internet set up," Ryann said. "Then we won't have to wait on the mail."

"I don't know," Mackenzie began. "I think there's something special about receiving a handwritten note in the mail."

"You're absolutely right, Mack." Zena put her hand on Mackenzie's. "There certainly is."

"Open it, Paige," Kayleigh said, just as excited as everyone else.

Paige began opening it. "Wait, where's Mercedes? We have to all be together."

Ryann shrugged her shoulders. "She sent me a text this morning saying she had a family emergency come up and that she wouldn't be here. I imagine it's something with Annie."

"Mercedes texts?" Paige had never seen or heard of Mercedes using text over voice. Mercedes always thought texting was impersonal and rude She hardly ever commented on their group texts. "That's strange."

"Stranger things have happened, I'm sure," Zena said

"I don't know..." Paige threw out her opinion.

"Read the letter from Angela, for Pete's sake!" Ryann said anxiously.

"Okay! Okay!" Paige carefully released the seal and pulled out a card.

"Oh!" Mackenzie sighed. "She made a card."

"Or at least attempted to," Paige said as she picked up a couple of the adornments that had not been affixed securely enough.

"It's the thought that counts," Mackenzie smiled.

"'Dear bestest friends,'" Paige began. "'As you can see, I attempted to make a homemade card. I thought Mack might be proud of my efforts.'"

The ladies all laughed, knowing craftiness was not one of Angela's talents.

Paige continued. "'Everything here in Africa is going well. We are slowly but surely getting settled. We've both been by ourselves for so long, it's going to take some time getting used to sharing space with someone else. I have already been to the orphanage. There are so many children who need homes. I wish I could adopt them all, but Tom says I can't, for more reasons than it's simply not possible. I imagine Paige is reading this while you all sit around the table listening. That's what I'm thinking about as I write. Words cannot express how much I miss you all. We'll have Internet soon and it will be much easier to keep in touch. Hug each other for me and it will seem as if I'm still there. Love to all, Angela.'"

"It will never seem like she's here again." Zena was sad.

"I read the other day that not feeling like you are socially connected to your friends makes you feel stupider and can even kill you," Paige spouted out.

Everyone looked at her, but there was complete silence.

Paige nodded her head in complete belief. "It's true I read it on the Internet."

Ryann snorted. "Well, if you saw it on the Internet it must be true."

Zena

"Oh!" Zena had almost forgotten. She held up her hand as she finished chewing and swallowing the food she had in her mouth. "This weekend. Fourth of July party at my house."

"Yay!" Paige sounded excited.

Zena didn't know what it was, but she felt as if she couldn't remember much of anything lately. Maybe it was adding the seventh child to her household. Maybe it was that her mind had been so excited about planning the shelter. Maybe it was her age; after all, she wasn't twenty years old anymore. In the end, she chalked it up to having too many things to remember and one of them was bound to get lost in the shuffle of life. At least that's what she told herself.

Their Fourth of July party was one of the most fun activities they hosted out on the farm. "So, who's coming?"

"Who's not coming?" Paige asked sarcastically.

Laughing, Zena scanned the table to see no raised hands. "All right. Maybe a better question is what are you all bringing?"

It was the one event where Zena allowed others to bring food to share. It made less work for her and allowed her more time to enjoy herself and her guests.

Everyone rattled off their offerings for the Fourth of July feast and the fun that would follow. Besides an enormous amount of food, there would be water balloons, water guns, yard games, pool fun, crafts, and of course fireworks. It really was the event of the summer that everyone looked forward to.

"Party starts at noon. Paige, feel free to come around eleven." Zena waited for Paige to react.

Paige just looked confused. "Why would I come an hour earlier than everyone else? Do you need help?" The way

Paige asked the question sounded like she was shocked that Zena, a.k.a. Martha Stewart, would need any preparation help.

Zena met Paige's eyes and held them hoping Paige would take note of the teasing twinkle. But she didn't.

All the other ladies at the table burst out laughing.

"What?" Paige looked even more confused.

"If she tells you an hour earlier, then maybe, just maybe, you'll be there on time," Ryann said.

"My money is on no she won't," Mackenzie commented matter-of-factly.

Zena laughed out loud as Paige scowled at Mackenzie first and then at Zena herself.

"You know I love you, Paige," Zena said, trying to ease Paige's torture.

"Mmmmm-hmmmm," was all Paige had to add.

Mercedes

Mercedes looked at the clock. The ladies would all be joining together in fellowship right about now. She just didn't have the strength mentally, emotionally, or physically. Everything that had gone on with Annie the last few weeks was truly wearing on her body and soul.

Not only had Annie made a lifestyle of bad decisions, but now her oldest daughter Alyssa was doing the same.

"Lord, I pray that you will help them see the error of their ways. I pray that You bring someone into their lives so they can learn and accept the truth. I know I'm not the one to try and convince them; I know how they feel about me. Anything I say will be considered preaching and push them away from you even farther. I pray that my life will be a testimony in and of itself. I pray that Your Word when spoken or lived out, will not return void."

Lately, Mercedes had felt so burdened to pray for her family, she felt it necessary to lay prostrate while she shared with God. This was only slightly better than kneeling, which had put great pressure and pain on her knees. Her body was quickly deteriorating, and she could certainly feel it.

Paige

Paige drove like a maniac. She was later than she had ever been. She had a really good excuse this time. Her brakes squealed as she pulled into Zena's driveway. Her contribution to the Fourth of July cookout was the hamburger and hot dog buns. With as late as she was, she figured everyone had already eaten the meat without the bread.

She ran into the back yard shouting, "I'm here! I'm here!" and holding up the grocery bags with the buns. "I'm sorry I'm late."

"What's your excuse this time?" Kayleigh wondered.

"Lose your car in the parking lot or something?" Mackenzie asked.

Paige thought both of them had suspicious-looking grins on their faces. "How did you know?

"You really lost your car in the parking lot?" Ryann asked.

"I did. I had to park in a different space because my usual area was full. When I came out, I couldn't find my car. I was walking back and forth between rows and up and down the aisles looking for my dumb car. It's only nine hundred degrees out here. Sweat was pouring off me so I probably smell bad now. I know everyone there was looking at me funny.

"I almost called one of you to come and help me. At least if we were driving up and down the aisles I wouldn't have looked so stupid. I thought my car was stolen. I was just about to call the police when this nice young man sensed my need for help. He helped me find my car. And why are you all grinning like fools?"

Movement from the back door caught her attention, and she looked up to see the nice young man who had helped her. She looked back at the ladies.

"I'd like you to meet Sam, Jocelyn's boyfriend," Ryann smiled. "He told us about some lunatic woman in the parking lot. We all bet it was you."

Everyone except Paige burst out laughing. As she plopped down in a chair by the pool and sulked. "I never liked you guys very much. I could have died out there in the sweltering heat and none of you would have cared."

"That isn't true, Paige. We love you and we do care. You look really hot, though. Do you need some cool water?" Mackenzie asked.

"That sounds lovely. At least you like me."

Paige's next words were literally drowned out as Mackenzie tipped the chair, sending Paige into the pool.

After Paige came up sputtering and maybe even swearing, everyone else jumped into the pool as well, clothes and all.

Zena

After everyone had eaten their fill, Zena stepped into the house to put leftovers away and wash the few dishes they used that couldn't be thrown away. She had shoved everyone else out of the kitchen and told them to go and enjoy

175

themselves, promising she would be finished in no more than five minutes.

She could not help but smile. Hosting others made her happy. Having her best friends and their families all together in one place made it that much sweeter.

Thank You, my precious Savior, for the blessings You continually bestow on me!

"Mom, can I tell everyone about our trip to the conservatory?" One of her littles, Zoe, had come into the kitchen.

Not really hearing the question, Zena replied with, "Whatever you want, sweetheart."

Shaking her head to bring herself back to the moment so she could complete her chores and return to the party, Zena finished in no time. Her attention was suddenly drawn outside when she heard nothing. No talking. No splashing in the pool. Thinking something was wrong, she grabbed a dish towel to dry her wet hands as she walked out onto the back deck.

She inwardly groaned when she saw the cause of the silence. Zoe held everyone's rapt attention as she gave a full report of what they had learned on a field trip to the observatory the other day. Zoe was just finishing her monologue, complete with highfaluting vocabulary, to which everyone gave a rousing round of applause.

When the clapping died down, Zena put her hands on Zoe's shoulders and said, "And that, my friends, concludes this audition for weird homeschoolers."

Everyone laughed and continued with what they were doing before Zoe held them captive.

Kayleigh

Kayleigh sat and enjoyed the evening. Jeff was out of town on business. She knew he was more than likely out drinking on this holiday and who knew what else, but she wasn't even sure she cared. He wasn't home. He wasn't keeping her from being with her friends, and he wasn't waiting for his dinner. Even after his visits to church he didn't seem any better. If anything, his temper had gotten worse. She chose to relish the time she had away from him.

Her thoughts drifted as the delightful squeals of the kids caught her attention. Zena had given all the children canning jars to store the lightning bugs they were catching. Their giggles and childish chatter made Kayleigh smile, and the spark of the lightning bugs that eluded the children's capture only added to the fireworks celebration going on overhead.

But later that night, when Kayleigh pulled into her garage, she was admittedly disappointed to see her husband's truck already there.

She closed her eyes and sighed. "Lord, help me to be gracious. Give me strength to deal with whatever waits for me."

Dread flooded her heart as soon as she opened the kitchen door and saw Jeff sitting at the table in the dark as if he had been waiting for her. He had been. He had that anxious look about him that always made Kayleigh nervous. She tried to be cheerful, hoping that would calm his nerves. And hers as well.

"You're home early," she pasted on a smile. She hoped it sounded different than what her heart was feeling.

"We need to talk." His voice was demanding.

"Okay," Kayleigh answered quietly.

"Have a seat," he demanded again. "Please," he added unexpectedly.

Kayleigh was halfway to sitting but stopped at the please. She just looked at him, unsure of how to respond. He never politely requested anything.

He nodded his head and held out his hand telling her to sit down the rest of the way.

Kayleigh stared. There was something different about him. Something she didn't recognize. Something that hadn't been there before.

"I've been under some…ah…conviction lately," he began. "I think that's what you call it. It's either that or a Jiminy Cricket moment."

Kayleigh chose not to speak. This was all too strange. She began to wonder if Jeff had started taking drugs on top of his drinking and carousing.

"I don't really understand it. All I can say is that this morning while I was doing some mundane work, my life flashed before my eyes, so to speak. At first I saw myself as a child. I saw old scenes of my father and how he treated me. How he treated my mom." He looked directly at Kayleigh. "Don't worry. I'm not going to give you all the gory details."

The only response Kayleigh gave was a slight smile.

"Picture after picture came to my mind until I thought I was going crazy. Then I remembered one evening in particular. I was hiding under my bed, listening to sounds no child should ever hear. I was scared to death. In fact, death seemed to be hanging over me. I had a feeling that one of us was going to die that night. I just wasn't sure if it was going to be my mom or me."

Jeff got up and got a glass of water. Kayleigh still sat silently, completely unsure of how to behave in this new situation in her marriage. Jeff downed the entire glass of water before he came back to sit in his seat and continue with his narrative.

"While I lay under my bed that night, I prayed. I prayed for the first time in my life. I'm not even sure where the idea to pray even came from. We never went to church. I never saw either of my parents pray. I don't even remember them mentioning God. But under my bed that night I prayed that God would save me and my mom. I begged God to help us. I even promised to never treat my wife like my father treated my mom."

Jeff stopped. Kayleigh could tell he wasn't quite finished, but that he needed to sort his thoughts.

Before speaking again, Jeff grabbed both of Kayleigh's hands in his. She winced.

"I didn't keep my promise. See, you are afraid, even by me touching your hands. I may not have done the things to you that my dad did to my mom, but I haven't treated you the way you deserve either."

Kayleigh took a chance and looked up into Jeff's eyes, although she wasn't quite sure what she would find there. She hoped this wasn't a cruel joke and Jeff was baiting her.

When she peered into his eyes, she saw no baiting. She knew that look well enough. That look could be one of pure evil, especially if he had been drinking. She began blinking quickly when she saw an actual tear roll down the side of Jeff's face.

He took a deep breath and squeezed her hands perhaps a little harder than Kayleigh would have liked, but she didn't withdraw them.

"I'm trying to say I'm sorry for all the pain and hurt I caused you. I'm sorry I've been a lousy husband. I'm sorry I haven't been there for you as you've been here for me, in spite of myself. I'd like to start our relationship over, and I want to do everything right this time."

He stopped talking and looked her in the eyes.

Kayleigh stared back.

After a minute he said, "Say something."

"I...I...I," Kayleigh stuttered. "I don't really know what to say."

"I know I probably caught you off guard."

Kayleigh bobbed her head back and forth. "You can say that again."

"I want to start over," he repeated. "Will you let me just court you like people used to do in the old days?"

"We're already married."

"Yes, but I want to create all new memories for you. I don't want to give you cause to leave me. At least not any more than I already have."

"I never had any intentions of leaving you."

With Kayleigh's declaration, a flood of tears burst forth from Jeff's eyes. He pushed his chair back from the table and fell on his knees before Kayleigh. He buried his head in her lap and sobbed like a hurting child, which Kayleigh now realized he truly was.

Tentatively at first, she put her hand on his head and smoothed his hair as a loving mother would have done.

In that moment she realized she had never known much about his childhood. He had told her early in their dating days that his parents were dead. After that, she never gave them much thought, if any at all.

Remembering her prayer in the car before she came into the house, she offered a prayer of thanksgiving. She had not been sure what to expect when she first saw Jeff's car, but this certainly wasn't it.

She looked down at his head, still in her lap, his arms wrapped around her, still repeating he was sorry over and over. She noticed a few gray hairs had popped out since their wedding day. Many things had changed, and Kayleigh had a feeling more changes were to come. In that moment she realized she was falling in love with her husband all over again.

Mackenzie

Cameron had had a hard day. He was finally asleep in Mackenzie's arms. She knew she should put him down so she could get some rest herself, but she just couldn't let him go.

She felt convicted that she hadn't prayed in quite a while, but she also felt it was useless. Then she thought of Kayleigh and her little black book. Kayleigh was a true prayer warrior. She never stopped praying. She was a testament to the fact that God always answers prayers. That was something Mackenzie believed deep down inside; maybe that was the problem. Maybe she was afraid of the answer God would send when she prayed. Would He answer with a big fat no to Cameron's healing?

With Cameron still asleep in her arms, Mackenzie bowed her head and closed her eyes. Her lips moved to the words that were running through her mind, but her voice was silent.

"God, here I am. I don't know what to do. I don't know what to say. You know my heart's desire. I need my little boy to be well. I need to see him jump and play like other kids without getting so tired. I don't understand why You're punishing him for my mistakes. I know I've made some bad decisions in my life, but none of them are his fault."

A tear dropped from the end of her chin and fell onto Cameron's cheek. Sniffling, Mackenzie gently wiped it away. An image from her childhood suddenly came to mind. It was a picture that had hung on the wall of her Sunday school classroom. It was a picture of God with His back turned on His Son as Jesus hung on the cross. God was weeping and His tears were falling like rain. In that moment, Mackenzie realized something she had known for years in her head, but it had now made it to her heart. God had given up His Son for all so that no one would have to pay the penalty for their sins.

Another father-son image came to her mind. This one of Abraham and Isaac. Abraham had been willing to give up his son if that was what God required of him.

Was God asking her if she was willing to give up her son? Cameron certainly could not save the world from sin, but could his life be a testimony to others? Was her response to his illness supposed to be a testimony to others as well?

So many questions, so few answers.

Mackenzie pulled Cameron a little closer to her chest. She closed her eyes and sat there allowing her heart to communicate with her heavenly Father.

After about fifteen minutes and a flood of tears, she relinquished control.

"He's Yours, Lord. Do with him as You please. Just please don't leave me to handle whatever it is You choose by myself."

Chapter 12

As iron sharpens iron, so one person sharpens another. - Proverbs 27:17

August

Kayleigh

Kayleigh was helping a customer when she felt the phone in her pocket vibrate. Her employer didn't mind if they kept their phones on them, but the devices needed to be left on silent and never pulled out if there were customers in the store. Kayleigh usually kept hers in her purse. The only people who tried to contact her during the day were the lunch ladies. Even that was all group texting silliness that Kayleigh could catch up with later. For some reason, she felt the need to keep her phone close to her today. Still, she had to wait for the customer she was helping to leave before she could look at it.

She discreetly closed her eyes and shook her head to try and bring herself back to her senses. She had no idea why she was feeling so anxious.

It wasn't until her lunch break when she was tucked away in the back room eating that she could look at her phone. Jeff's name flashed across the screen, and she felt her stomach plummet to her feet. She pushed her food away. Suddenly, she wasn't hungry.

Taking a deep breath, she opened the text.

I'm very serious about restoring our relationship. Can I take you out on a date tonight?

Kayleigh didn't know what to think or how to respond. While she was thinking another text came in from Jeff.

I know this probably sounds silly, but I don't want to be intimate with you, so there are no expectations for tonight. I want to start over for real. I want to earn back your love. I want you to want to be with me sexually, not just do it because you're afraid of what I might do if you don't.

That didn't make things any easier. This was certainly not the Jeff she had come to know.

"What should I do, Lord?" She silently prayed hoping for a quick response.

She felt something, or maybe it was Someone, telling her to go. Maybe what she had been praying for the last several years was finally being answered. If that was the case then she needed to trust God. Even if it scared her.

Ok.

I'll pick you up at seven. Wear something nice.

Kayleigh couldn't remember the last time they went out someplace where she had to dress nicely. In fact, she couldn't remember the last time they went out at all. Maybe she would splurge and buy something new for the occasion. Suddenly hungry once again, she finished her lunch quickly so she could allow herself a few minutes to shop before she went back to work. It wouldn't take long. She knew exactly what dress she was going to buy.

Later that evening, at precisely 7 o'clock the doorbell rang. Scrunching her eyebrows together she went to answer. Jeff stood there holding a dozen peach roses. She smiled realizing he had never forgotten her favorites.

"May I come in?" he asked as he handed her the flowers.

Playing along, Kayleigh accepted the flowers and stood aside so he could enter.

He gave her a chaste kiss on the cheek. "You look just as beautiful as the day I first saw you."

Kayleigh felt herself blush. When was the last time he had spoken to her like that?

"You don't look so bad yourself," she smiled. He must have gone out and bought a new suit for himself. That explained why he had not come home after work.

That evening was one of the best Kayleigh ever had with Jeff. True to his word, Jeff didn't expect or ask anything further from Kayleigh. As they prepared for bed, Jeff took her face in his hands and kissed her on the forehead. Kayleigh thought it was the sweetest kiss she had ever received. Ever.

She rolled over onto her side away from Jeff as a tear rolled down her cheek. It wasn't a tear of sadness. It was one of thankfulness, love, and hope.

∞ ∞ ∞

Mercedes

Mercedes didn't feel like talking to anyone, especially to any of the lunch ladies. They knew her too well. Instead of talking, she opted to send Ryann a text, her second one in two months. She was surprised no one had said anything to her after the last one. Of course, she had pretty much kept away from them all. She had shown her face just enough to keep the gossip down.

Going to miss lunch today, sorry. Things will be settled soon.

She hoped that was enough to keep Ryann happy and unconcerned.

Of course, she also knew she wasn't being fair to her friends. She sighed as a text came through from Ryann.

I hope so.

Then her phone rang. The text from Ryann distracted her. She never meant to answer calls.

"Hello?" She cringed as soon as she said it.

"What's really going on?" It was Ryann. "And don't just tell me it's a family problem. I want details."

"I just can't." Mercedes never was very good at lying.

"Mercy, spill the beans. What's going on with you? We've been friends for a long time, you can tell me anything. I have a feeling there's more to it than Annie."

"I'm dying."

Ryann didn't say anything at first. Mercedes began to wonder if the call had been disconnected, and she looked at her phone to make sure.

"What?" Ryann whispered. "How long have you known?"

"For about a year."

"Why didn't you say anything?"

"I didn't want anyone to look at me or treat me any differently. I wanted to enjoy the time I had living my life to the fullest, not being pitied."

"Maybe the doctor is wrong. They've been wrong before."

"No. The cancer came back, and it has spread to my other organs."

"Can you get some treatments?"

Mercedes shook her head. "No. I'm beyond treatments."

"Really?"

"Well, I mean I could, but then my quality of life wouldn't be worth it, not for the length of time it would give me. I don't want to be a burden to anyone."

"Oh, Mercy!" Ryann could tell she was crying. "You wouldn't be a burden to anyone. You could move in with me, and I'll take care of you like you did me."

"I'm not sure there's enough time for me to pack up and move."

"Really?" Ryann whispered again. "How long?" she choked out.

"Thirty days."

Mercedes just listened to Ryann cry. She hated this. Why couldn't Ryann just have left her alone to die in peace?

"We're going to have lunch every week, and you're going to come to all of them. I'm picking you up in an hour. Be sure you're ready."

"I don't want to go, Ryann," Mercedes said.

"What if it's the last time you are able to come eat with us?"

Mercedes took a deep breath. "All right I'll be ready."

"Good."

"Ryann, wait. Ryann?" Mercedes looked at the screen of her phone to see that the call had ended.

Paige

"It's good to know someone's kids are perfect," Paige said watching Zena's children. "I mean they sit and eat all of their food, and then they clean up their mess without being told." She looked at Zena before adding her expected jab. "You just have the perfect life, don't you?"

"I think we've already been over that," was all Zena said.

As soon as the words were out of Paige's mouth, she knew she had once again said the wrong thing, or maybe the right thing in the wrong way?

"I'm sorry, Zena," she apologized.

Zena waved her off. "My kids sit and eat like that because they're so many of them. If they get up and leave their plate of food, it won't be there when they get back. Someone else will see it as fair game. It's happened before."

Paige smiled. She was glad Zena wasn't mad at her. She was reminded of all the years she was robbed of having a sibling. She wished she and Tom had been able to grow up in the same household. Having siblings must have been wonderful. Maybe Tom would have taught her what to say and what not to say.

"Oh goodness!"

Kayleigh's voice pulled Paige out of her thoughts. She looked up to see Ryann helping Mercedes walk across the park.

"She looks horrible!" Immediately Paige cringed. She had done it once again. When would she ever learn to control the runway between her brain and her mouth?

Mackenzie

Mackenzie turned her head toward the parking lot to see what all the commotion was about. She saw Mercedes shake her head and Ryann turn her around and go back in the direction of the car. Mackenzie jumped up and ran toward them.

"What's the matter?"

"I'm having some small health issues of my own," Mercedes said, to which Ryann snorted.

"You're going to tell everyone the truth." Ryann had suddenly taken on the role of mother instead of the other way around.

Mackenzie watched as Ryann helped Mercedes get back in her car. Mackenzie wasn't going back to the group at the picnic table until she knew all the details of what was going on with Mercedes. She climbed into the backseat of the car and scooched toward the middle so she could lean over the console.

"What's the matter, Mercedes?" she demanded.

Before Mercedes could answer, the rest of the group was opening doors from both sides and cramming into the car.

"What's going on?" asked Kayleigh.

"What are you guys doing?" Ryann addressed the group.

"Is this where the party is?" Paige wondered.

"Where are the kids?" Mackenzie asked Zena.

"I've given instructions to my oldest and Jordan. Don't worry. They're all in good hands. What's happening in here?"

"Not breathing!" Paige said as she rearranged herself to sit on Mackenzie's lap.

"What is it, Mercy?" Although Mackenzie's voice was quiet, it reverberated through the car and everyone quit the chatter and looked to Mercedes for answers.

Mackenzie could tell Mercedes was struggling to breathe, and not because of the amount of oxygen left in the car.

"I'm not going to be with you much longer. I've been sick for quite some time, and I feel that God will be calling me home soon."

Voices in the car erupted with questions once again. With seemingly great difficulty, Mercedes held up her hand for silence.

"I don't really want to talk about it. It tires me too much. Ryann knows the facts, and she can share them with you later. Let's just enjoy our time together."

More silence followed. Mackenzie figured everyone felt the same emotion she was feeling - shock. But she would respect Mercedes' wishes and not talk about it. At least not now. Ryann would definitely be getting a phone call later.

Zena

Zena's phone rang. The timing could not have been more perfect. She grabbed it excitedly and said, "Oh, you guys, I have a surprise for you!"

She fumbled with her phone a moment before shouting, "Hello!"

"Why are you shouting at me?" It was Angela's voice which made everyone else in the car shout.

Zena passed her phone off to Ryann who was sitting in the middle of the front seat. "Hold it up so she can see all of us."

Ryann did as she was told.

"Why are you guys all crammed into one car?" Angela asked.

"Mercedes is feeling a little under the weather, so we decided to have our picnic lunch in the car."

"Sounds a little..." She paused, apparently looking for the right word.

"Cramped?" Paige helped her out.

"But there are no ants, and if it rains, we don't have to worry about getting wet," Kayleigh was her always encouraging self.

"Why didn't you sit in Zena's van? It has a lot more space." When no one responded, she asked, "Why do you guys look all depressed? You're giving me a complex for calling," Angela said.

Zena looked to Ryann for the answer. Apparently, she was the only one besides Mercedes who knew the truth. Zena noticed a look pass between Ryann and Mercedes, Mercedes giving a slight nod of her head.

Before speaking, Ryann took a deep breath. "Mercedes has some pretty severe health issues, and I'm afraid she won't be with us much longer."

"What?" Angela gasped.

Ryann spoke quickly as if she would lose her nerve if she didn't. Zena could hear Ryann's voice trying to stay strong but breaking down just the same.

"She's known about the cancer for a while now, but she didn't say anything because she didn't want us fools treating her any differently."

Zena knew Ryann's use of the word "fools" was meant to add a little humor to a devastating situation. It didn't help much.

Ryann continued speaking after grabbing and squeezing Mercedes' hand and looking her in the eye. "We both know how overzealous this group can be."

When no one said anything for about thirty seconds, Mercedes spoke up. "This is what I don't want. Can we all just pretend to be normal? Angela, we need to talk about the good things that are going on in your life."

"How is everything?"

"We miss you!"

"When are you coming home?"

The ladies all began to speak at once.

"Whoa!" Angela held up her hand. "One at a time."

"How are you?" Mackenzie repeated her question from the back seat.

"It's more wonderful than I ever dreamed!"

"Are you pregnant yet?" Paige voiced her question before anyone else had a chance to say anything.

Everyone in the car turned to stare her down.

Angela was the one to break the silence. "Uhhhh...no."

They chatted a while longer.

When Zena noticed that Mercedes looked extremely tired, she ended the call. Zena couldn't help but wonder what the new normal without both Angela and Mercedes would look like. She already wasn't a fan.

"Whew! Fresh air!" Paige commented as she stepped out of the car.

"Now I know how clowns feel when they are all piled into a car at the circus," Mackenzie added.

Zena smiled at their comments, but her thoughts and her sights were on Mercedes. She climbed back into the front seat and put her hand on Mercedes' arm.

Mercedes turned her head to look at Zena.

"You know we all love you."

Mercedes smiled. "You guys are the best," she whispered hoarsely.

Kayleigh

Kayleigh rolled over in bed with a smile on her face. Lately, her first thoughts of the day were, "Thank You, Lord!" She felt like a teenager in love again, only it was different this time. It was true love, not infatuation. The last few weeks with Jeff had been all that she had hoped her marriage would be. She had been leery at first, but she knew Jeff couldn't keep up an act like this. It was real. He was truly repentant for all he had done to her. He was changing. The only way it could have happened was because of God. All of her prayers were being answered and God had become a part of Jeff's life.

Her mind wandered back to the previous evening.

Jeff had put a lot of thought into the date. They had taken a walk at the park, went to a pizza place for dinner, and then went to the movies. It was an older movie they had seen before, but she had always liked it when the local theater pulled out some old reels.

"Does any of this bring back memories?" Jeff asked as they walked home hand-in-hand.

Kayleigh shrugged her shoulders. "I remember seeing that movie before."

"Do you remember when?"

It took her a moment, but then she asked, "Did we see it together?"

"Yep. On our very first date."

Kayleigh's mind drifted back in years as she tried to conjure up the night of their first date. It didn't take her long to realize the entire evening had been a replica of their first date. The park. The pizzeria. Even the movie. How had she forgotten when he remembered everything?

Her smile took over her entire face as she looked up at him. It was in that moment she realized he truly did love her and that he was working on overcoming his struggles. It was also the moment she was able to let her guard down and be herself again. The tension she hadn't realized was there, melted away. It was then that she knew their marriage was going to make it.

Jeff had kept his word about their courting relationship. He had not once pressured her into intimacy, but when she had made the suggestion last night, he made sure she was ready. He made sure it was because she wanted to, not because she felt she had to.

It had been... Well, she wasn't one to kiss and tell, but another, "Thank You, Lord," escaped her lips.

Just then Jeff rolled over and draped his arm around her. "Good morning."

"Good morning," Kayleigh smiled back.

"I think we might need a repeat of last night sometime soon."

Kayleigh laughed as she held him tight. Apparently, the evening had been memorable for him as well. She would be more than willing to oblige.

∞ ∞ ∞

Mackenzie

Mackenzie's face hurt from so much smiling lately. Cameron had been seeing the specialist for only about a month, and there had already been great improvement in his health. From the first visit, Mackenzie felt Cameron was finally where he needed to be. On the first visit, the doctor had Cameron laughing as he searched Cam's body for any clues as to his illness. The doctor had studied Cam's records, including all the tests he had previously had.

"There's no need to redo tests that are not necessary, especially the ones that cause the poor little guy pain."

Mackenzie had never been so pleased with the medical care Cameron was receiving.

It didn't take too long for the doctor to find a possible cause for all the problems.

"How long has this been here?" he asked as he searched Cameron's head.

Mackenzie leaned over and looked at what he was pointing at. "What is that?" It looked like a perfect bull's-eye.

"It looks like a tick bite."

Mackenzie was confused. "When would he have been bitten by a tick? I thought they were only in the woods or tall weeds."

"The doctor shrugged his shoulders. "Not necessarily. The last couple of years have been bad. It could've come into your house on you or anyone that visited. Dogs are especially noted for carrying ticks into a home."

"We don't have a dog."

"Anyway, Lyme disease would explain just about all of his symptoms. The fever, the flu symptoms. I think his joints were aching when he told you that his knee hurt."

"What about slapping his leg?"

The doctor smiled knowingly. "We often slap our arms, legs, hands, feet, whatever part of our body that falls asleep. I think it was a natural reaction to tingling."

At first, Mackenzie felt ashamed that number one, she had allowed Cameron to be bitten by a tick, and number two, that she never noticed the spot on his head for all the times she washed his hair.

"Don't be so hard on yourself," the doctor said. "A lot of people miss it, especially when the bite is on the scalp. Hair covers it up."

Since starting on some new medications, Cameron was becoming more active. More like any two, almost three-year-old. Yes, his becoming more active was more work for Mackenzie, but she loved it. She might go to bed absolutely exhausted, but she wouldn't have it any other way.

Before falling into a deep sleep, she sat up in bed to pray.

"Lord, thank You for Your grace. I don't deserve anything You've given me. I thank You for putting Your hand on Cameron and bringing a doctor into his life that truly cared enough to take time with him and find the answers I've needed for so long. Thank You for giving me my son back. Amen."

She slept soundly that night as one who was completely at peace.

∞ ∞ ∞

Kayleigh

Kayleigh knew it was late, but she felt an urgency to talk with Zena. She could see a light on toward the back of the house, so instead of ringing the doorbell and disrupting the entire household, she lightly knocked on the door. She saw Zena poke her head out of the lit up room. Kayleigh waved.

As soon as Zena opened the door, she pulled Kayleigh inside. "What is it?" she asked. "Is that loser hurting you again?"

It was then that Kayleigh realized Zena had not seen "that loser" standing behind her. She smiled as she responded. "No, but we both want to talk to you."

Zena looked a little suspicious. "Should I get Cooper?"

"Maybe. This would involve him too."

At the sound of his name, Cooper appeared behind Zena. "Is everything all right?"

Kayleigh smiled again. "Everything is good."

Zena invited them in and offered refreshment, which they declined.

"You know things have been going pretty well for us lately." Kayleigh started right into why they were there.

"We've been praying for a ministry to do together and you and your shelter keep coming to mind. Both our minds. You know Jeff is a psychologist. The women that come here are going to need some counseling, someone to talk to. Who better than us?"

Kayleigh got a little nervous when Zena didn't say anything right away, but then Jeff spoke up.

"Don't think you have to come up with an answer right away. We want you to take the time to talk and pray about it together."

Then Zena smiled and nodded. "I don't even have all the details worked out for myself yet. I don't know how or even if any of this will work."

"I feel so strongly about this that it must have come from the Lord," Kayleigh said.

Zena sighed. "I know you don't take things of God lightly." She glanced at Jeff. "You're proof of that."

Kayleigh watched as Cooper took Zena's hand and said, "Honey, let's just take some time to pray as they suggested. This whole shelter idea is no small thing, but I know it's something you've had on your heart for quite some time, and I also know it's desperately needed."

Zena took a deep breath and held it for a moment. She then nodded her head. "We'll pray."

Kayleigh could not help but jump up with excitement. The way she and Jeff had come up with the same idea at the same time could only have come from God. Grabbing Zena's hands, she said, "Thank you!" Kayleigh was afraid to say anything else for fear that the tears might start flowing. Not that Zena would care. They would have cried together. That's what friends did.

Ryann knew the vigil would be long and short at the same time. Long, because she was waiting for her friend to die. Short, because she was waiting for her friend to die. Ryann had moved in with Mercedes the previous week. Jocelyn knew it was important for Ryann to be with Mercedes and had offered to hold down the fort at home. Mercedes had been there for Ryann when life was difficult; there was no way Ryann would not have been there for her in her most desperate times.

While Mercedes had not divulged all the details surrounding Annie, Ryann could deduce the relationship had suffered immensely. When Ryann had called Annie to inform her of her mother's deteriorating condition, Annie had all but hung up on her. That was when Ryann made the decision to move in with Mercedes. There was no way one of her very best friends in the entire world was going to die without a loved one by her side.

Mercedes had made all of her own funeral arrangements and paid for them.

"One of the benefits of knowing you're dying soon," Mercedes tried to crack a joke.

But it wasn't funny.

Ryann was grateful Mercedes had already taken care of her final plans. After her husband was killed in the accident Ryann was left to do everything herself. Definitely not a job she relished. It was a lesson learned though. Shortly after his funeral, Ryann made all the plans for her own so that her girls wouldn't be left with that devastating task. Jocelyn had a key to the little safe Ryann had bought to hold all her important documents. In spite of the morbidity of it all, she was glad it was done.

Mercedes' ragged breathing intruded on Ryann's thoughts. When the doctor had stopped by earlier, that was one of the symptoms he said to look for. She felt her own breathing take a definite change. Then she felt her face flush and her entire body go numb.

Picking up her phone, she sent the text no one ever wanted to receive. The one consolation was that she and Mercedes both would be surrounded by comforting hearts soon.

Kayleigh

The bright, blinking light of her cell phone going off woke Kayleigh. She squinted to see the time of the clock. 3:30 AM. She had taken to leaving her phone on in case Mercedes' condition worsened. Kayleigh picked up her phone, almost afraid to read the text that had come in.

Went into a coma. It probably won't be long now.

Kayleigh realized she must have slept through at least the first several texts because of the responses.

She texted back. *I'll be there in a few.*

"Everything okay," Jeff said as he rolled closer to her. Kayleigh handed him her phone. She wasn't sure she could say the words out loud. The next thing she knew, Jeff was also out of bed.

"I'm sorry I woke you."

"I'm not," he smiled. "I'm going with you."

The changes in Jeff were still so new that Kayleigh wasn't quite sure how to respond. "Oh, that isn't necessary."

"I want to."

"What about work?"

He shrugged his shoulders. "I have days I need to take off anyway."

"I don't know how long I'll be."

Jeff stepped up to her, put his hands on her shoulders, and said, "I haven't been a very good husband to you, but I'm trying now. I can be a designated driver of sorts if you or any of your friends don't feel like driving home later."

Kayleigh speechlessly stared into his eyes. Her tears started to fall. "Thank you," was all she could manage to whisper.

Jeff kissed her hand before letting her go to get himself dressed.

When Jeff turned back around to look at her, she said, "I love you."

He smiled back. "I know. And I'm trying to be better at showing my love for you."

By the time Kayleigh and Jeff arrived, everyone else was already there.

They all sat in chairs around the bed, each with a hand on Mercedes.

"Can we pray?" Kayleigh felt an overwhelming need to talk to God, not for Mercedes, but for those who would remain after she was gone.

The ladies all nodded and Kayleigh began. "Lord, we come before You today because we are hurting. We put Mercedes in Your hands. I pray that she is in no pain. Please don't allow her to suffer."

When she paused, another one took up the vigil. Eventually, they made their way all around the bed. That was when Kayleigh felt the slightest of squeezes on her hand. She looked up cautiously so as not to disturb the others, but she couldn't help but gasp when she noticed Mercedes looking directly at her.

Mercedes

Mercedes opened her eyes to see the lunch ladies surrounding her. She had dreamed of seeing the Lord, and she knew that dream would soon be a reality. Kayleigh sat next to her, holding her hand. Mercedes gave it a squeeze and said, "I want to go home." That was all she had the strength for, but she knew her closest friends in the entire world would understand her meaning. Her body was tired. There was no longer any fight left in her. It was time.

Chapter 13

A sweet friendship refreshes the soul. - Unknown

September

Paige
(From the blog)

I know I normally write about romantic relationships, but today I want to talk about a different kind of relationship: friendship.

Friendship is truly one of God's greatest gifts. Some friends come into our lives and are only there for a short time. Other friends are there for the long haul. Some people are forgotten almost as soon as they are out of our lives. Others leave an impression that will always be a part of us. I mean *FOREVER* a part of us.

My friend, Mercedes, is one of these people. I first met her when I was about twenty, but we truly got to know each other and grow close over the last five years. Her nickname is Mercy, although she hates to be called that. It's the perfect description of who she is. She shows mercy to all with whom she comes in contact, especially me! I have a habit of blurting out whatever comes to my mouth. My tongue is moving and biting before my brain has a chance to think. Mercedes has helped me with that. I think that's part of the reason I enjoy blogging. I can delete anything that shouldn't be said before I publish to live.

Mercedes is a walking example of how God treats us. We don't deserve anything from Him, but He gave everything.

Mercedes always gives her all. Mercedes will always hold a special place in my heart.

Mackenzie

Mackenzie looked at herself in the full-length mirror adjusting anything that needed adjusting and making sure all her layers were in their proper place. The garments women tortured themselves with to try and look halfway decent were astounding. And uncomfortable. But wearing overly tight spandex was slightly better than trying to remember to suck everything in all the time. Sucking in her fat was not what she wanted to remember today.

"I suppose I should go check on the boys and see if they've torn off their suits yet." Mackenzie spoke to her reflection.

Giving her black dress one last glance she looked out of the room and down the stairs to where she had left the boys watching TV. They were all getting settled nicely into Angela's house. The boys were thoroughly enjoying the backyard. Mackenzie felt that she would forever be in Angela's debt.

Partly because of their living arrangements, things were starting to look up for her and her little family. Her new job was going amazingly well. The company offered her great benefits that kicked in immediately. Mackenzie could see a definite glow to Cameron's little boy cheeks that had not been there before. She loved the faint pink that should have been there all along. It was one of those things she hadn't noticed was missing until it was there. What was ahead, she still wasn't sure, but she had learned to put it all in God's capable hands where it always should have been. Maybe that was what God had been asking of her all along, to put her complete faith and trust in Him.

Leaning against the doorframe, she stood there and watched. Thankfully, the boys had obeyed and not ruined their clothes while she was getting ready. They sat in the middle of the couch together; Jordan had his arm around Cameron's neck. What a great brother he was!

Mackenzie blinked a few times to try and stop the tears. There would be plenty of opportunity for tears later.

Paige

Paige was a mess and she knew it. She never even bothered applying any makeup. It was all just going to be washed off as she wiped away the constant barrage of tears. She didn't recall being this much of a mess when her own mother had died. Perhaps that was due to the fact that she was so young, or it could have been that she and her mom had never developed a relationship. Paige felt her bond with Mercedes had been much more like a mother-daughter relationship should have been, and Paige would miss it terribly.

Ryann

Ryann couldn't believe she was sitting here. She should be the one lying in the coffin at the front of the church. Mercedes had been Ryann's cheerleader the entire time she was going through her cancer treatments, the whole time she herself was dying.

Now that two members of the group were gone, Ryann didn't feel as if she wanted to continue planning the monthly lunches. It just wouldn't be the same without all of them together.

"Ryann?"

Ryann turned around to see the pastor standing behind her.

"Hi," Ryann said. She looked for more words but nothing came to mind. She felt a little numb.

"I, uh, have something for you." He held out an envelope.

"What is it?" Ryann asked, reaching out to take it.

"It's a letter."

"From who?"

"Mercedes."

"Oh."

"It's actually for all of you. Along with a box of stuff I have in my office. She requested you read the letter all together."

Ryann smiled, sort of. "We're all going over to Zena's afterward. I'll grab the box from your office before I leave."

He smiled a sad smile. "I'll leave the door unlocked for you."

"Thanks."

Kayleigh

Throughout the illness and loss of Mercedes, Kayleigh finally allowed herself to truly believe Jeff was a changed man. He had not only allowed her time to visit Mercedes as much as she could, but he also offered to drive her, cook at home, bring takeout to Mercedes' house, not that Mercedes was eating much. Jeff was thoughtful. He was taking care of Kayleigh and in a way he never had before.

"You need to eat to keep up your strength. You won't be any good to Mercy if you have no energy."

Many nights he had just held her and let her cry. He was sympathetic to her grief.

There were many other nights he had been the cause of Kayleigh's tears. In an effort to help Kayleigh understand, not condone, why he was the way he was, he shared story after brutal story about his childhood. He spoke of nights his drunken and/or high father had beaten him to within an inch of his life. The beatings explained many of the scars on Jeff's body that Kayleigh had never given much thought to before.

Now, when she had the opportunity, she caressed them with the tips of her fingers.

When they had arrived home after Mercedes' passing, Jeff held Kayleigh tightly as she sobbed harder than she had ever sobbed before. She had fallen asleep in his arms. When she awoke several hours later, she realized he had not made any effort to move or get more comfortable. In that moment it was all about Kayleigh. That was the moment Kayleigh realized their marriage would stand the test of time. If they could get through what they had already been through, nothing would tear them apart.

Zena

After the services, Zena arrived home before all of the other ladies got there. Ever since she had received word that Mercedes had left them, she had to keep busy. She offered to host everyone at her house after the funeral so they could all cry and reminisce. Because everyone was coming over, she had been baking and cooking for days. She honestly didn't know what she was going to do with all of it. Even her kids couldn't eat that much.

The air was so hot and oppressive. It felt strange. Zena had never felt anything like it before. In spite of the air conditioning being on, Zena needed to open a window or two. She didn't know what was wrong with her. She was too young for menopause to have kicked in.

As she looked out the window, she noticed the blue, cloudless sky and the bright sunshine. It almost felt as if a storm was coming, but the heavens gave no indication of that whatsoever.

"It feels weird outside today," Ryann had quietly come in and stood behind her.

At least Zena now knew it wasn't all in her head. "I thought it was just me."

"Your house is immaculate!" Kayleigh said when she walked in and gave Zena a hug. "Not that your house is ever a mess. At the same time, I've always felt it wasn't just a house, but a home."

"Thanks." Zena smiled. "Cleaning has been one of my 'have to keep busy' activities."

"Oh, Zena, it's so good to be back here!" Angela and Tom walked in next, their newly adopted daughter, Lily, with them.

Angela

It was good to be back home, but even holding her precious little girl couldn't take away the pain she was feeling after the loss of her friend. She watched Lily scamper about with Zena's children. Lily never failed to make Angela smile.

"Isn't it a little soon after your whirlwind romance to adopt?"

Angela didn't even mind Paige's comments. "Well, I'm not getting any younger. Besides, I want to be like my new sister-in-law and live life to the fullest." She smiled and winked at Paige.

Ryann

After everyone had arrived and when there was a lull in the conversation, Ryann spoke up. "I think we need to read Mercedes' letter. Paige, can you grab that box over there, please?"

Paige quietly did as she was asked.

When no one else said anything, Ryann opened the sealed envelope and pulled out several pages. Tears immediately came to her eyes when she saw the scraggly handwriting. Mercedes must have written the letter in her own hand even though she barely had the strength.

Mercedes' Letter

Here we are. At least here you are. I just wanted to say one last goodbye to let you know how much I love you all. In my recent downtime, I did a little research on the meaning behind your names. What I found was extremely interesting. It's proof to me that our parents really don't have a lot to say about our names, surprisingly. God has His hand even in that small detail of our lives.

Ryann, your name means "little leader." How appropriate is that for who you are! What a wonderful leader of our group of friends you have been. You are our rock. You are the glue that holds us all together. Without you there would have been no monthly lunches and probably no meaningful friendships. Thanks for the fellowship. I also imagine you are considering giving up the monthly lunches because the dynamics of the group are changing. I beg you not to. While some of us may have moved on in one way or another, there are many other women who need exactly what this group offers. Don't stop. Go out and find new people to lead and befriend. Open your hearts to them.

My gift for you is this heart locket. I wanted to put all of our faces in it so you could always keep all of us near to your heart, but for obvious reasons, I couldn't. You are truly the heart of our little group.

Mackenzie, your name has meaning that is just as appropriate. It means "teacher." You are always so willing to share your knowledge and creativity with others. I have loved your dry sense of humor. You made me laugh when I've been with you and later when I recall your comments. I want you to know I have truly treasured the framed scrapbook page. I hung it where I can see it every day. I have made one for you. It's not as good as any of yours, but it's a piece of me I hope you'll treasure. In the words of Winnie the Pooh, "If ever there is tomorrow when we're not together, there is something you must always remember. You are braver than you believe, stronger than you seem, and smarter than you think. But the most important thing is, even if we're apart, I'll always be with you." You are a tower of strength. Your testimony is one of God's love for His children.

Zena, as your name implies, you are the epitome of hospitality. I know you've been a cooking fool for at least a few days. That's how you take care of people you love, and that's one of the things I love about you, but it is your strength to rise up from adversity that I envy. Thank you for sharing your story with us this past year. I am not the same person for knowing it. You helped me learn to overcome my ailments. By the way, your scars are things of beauty. Christ has physical scars too. He wasn't afraid to show His; don't be afraid to show yours. Here's a cross necklace you can wear to proudly proclaim Christ for the women with whom you will work.

Angela, God knew from the time you were conceived that you would be an angel, a giver to many. Your generosity never ceases to amaze me. You show us all that the more one gives, the more God gives in return. I want to give you my watch. I know you've always liked it, and I want you to remember that God's timing is always perfect. Sometimes we have to wait on Him, even though the waiting can sometimes seem painful and long. He always has a plan. God has made your life one of beauty in His way and in His time. I don't think I ever saw you smile so much until you met Tom. I hope you keep smiling.

Kayleigh, what a prayer warrior and encourager you are. You may not know it, but you silently encouraged me to look for the good in people and see what they need is an encouraging word. I don't think you can ever realize how much your daily prayers meant to me. Here's a framed copy of Albrecht Durer's *Praying Hands*. Look up his story if you ever get a chance someday. Hang it in a prominent place in your home so you will constantly be reminded to pray, not that you need reminders. You have taken the verse, "Pray without ceasing" to a whole new level. Prayer warriors are few and far between these days, and I'm proud I have one I consider one of my very dearest friends.

Paige, you have such a servant's heart, truly living up to your name. I can't tell you the number of times you have come to me to fulfill a need I had told no one about. We might all tease you because of being late, but I know for a fact that some of those times were when you stopped to help someone else who needed it. That shows your servant's heart and that you always put the needs of others before your own. You listen to the voice of God and then take action. Keep living life to the fullest because tomorrow is never promised to any one of us. While there may be plenty of people here on earth who don't notice, remember that God does. Be a friend to many. I'm certain that when it's your turn to stand before the Throne of Grace you will certainly hear, "Well done, my good and faithful servant." My gift to you is an umbrella. Sounds silly, I know, but I want you to keep dancing in the rain.

I can't help but think of Jesus' disciples when I think of all of you. They were a pretty motley crew, much like us. They had nothing going for them and no political or social power of their own. However, with the help of the Holy Spirit, they were able to turn the world upside down. You have all turned my world upside down. Your love for God and the use of your talents for the Kingdom amaze me! Keep up the work of God, and keep turning people's worlds on end. Be His disciples. Show His love.

I recently came across a silly quiz in a teenage girl magazine. Since there was little else I was able to do at the time, I took the quiz. You know what I discovered? There was actually a lot of meat to that stupid quiz. This is how you know you have a friend that's worth keeping. These apply to each one of you.

A friend always has your back.

A friend is someone you can share everything with; the good, the bad, the ugly.

A friend proves that you are loved and cared about.

A friend can make you laugh at all the appropriate times, especially the times when you need to laugh.

A friend is always honest, even when it's hard.
A friend is trustworthy with everything.
A friend makes you feel comfortable.
A friend allows you to be yourself.
A friend cheers for you.
A friend encourages you.

Please don't cry for me. I am no longer in the pain and discomfort I carried for years. Think of the happy times, the funny times. Always be merciful and loyal to each other and others you meet. Don't ever give up praying for each other. No matter where you all end up in the world, no matter how many miles there may be between you, when you come together in prayer you are an unbroken circle.

One more thing, I took some notes from Mackenzie and made a collage. See, Mack, I'm not hopeless! This collage contains pictures of many of our times together. If you look closely, you'll notice that all of us are smiling in every picture. That's how I want you to be. When you think of me, always be smiling. When you think of each other, always smile.

Take turns hanging this collage in each of your homes. Study the faces while thinking about the lives each one represents. Pray for each other daily. Love each other. Be there for each other

I love you all. Goodbye for now, Mercedes.

Ryann

The curtain to Ryann's left lifted as if by a brisk breeze, but Ryann neither felt a breeze nor noticed any leaves on the trees right outside the window move. She set the letter on her lap and said, "Goodbye, my friend."

About the Author

Ruth O'Neil was born and raised in upstate New York and attended Houghton College. She and her high school sweetheart have been married since 1991 and reside in Virginia. She has been a freelance writer/editor for more than twenty years and has published hundreds of articles in dozens of publications. Besides freelancing, she has written two stand-alone novels in the What a Difference a Year Makes series (*Come Eat at My Table* and *Belonging),* numerous devotionals, and a couple of children's picture books. She is the author of the Spiritual Insights from the Classics series, which are devotional companions to classic literature. Books in this series include devotional companions for *Little Women, Wizard of Oz, 20,000 Leagues Under the Sea, Charlotte's Web, A Wrinkle in Time,* and *The Hound of the Baskervilles.*

Ruth also teaches Writer's Forums to help want-to-be authors break into print with either freelancing or book publishing.

She is a veteran homeschool mom, teaching her kids at home for 20 years. Several years ago she began teaching writing classes at a local homeschool co-op. Here she now teaches younger writers to develop their own freelancing career, write their own novel, or create their own picture book. Teaching the next generation of writers is probably the most fun she's ever had!

When she's not writing or teaching, Ruth spends her time cooking for others, quilting, reading, scrapbooking, camping, and hiking with her family.

You can find Ruth at ruthoneil.weebly.com.